THIS SUMMER AT THE LAKE

DAPHNE JAMES HUFF

for Adrianna

THE INKY BLACK canvas of the Montana night sky was broken only by the lights on Logan's bike. He knew he would miss the silence once he got to New York, but right now, it was the last thing he wanted to hear. He longed for the excitement of the city, even though he'd never been anywhere bigger than Billings. He'd never even been outside of Montana.

His entire life, Logan had been listening to tourists from all over talk about how beautiful his home state was. Flathead Lake, especially. This summer he was finally eighteen, and old enough to be a server. Instead of hearing snippets of conversations as he bused tables, he could actually ask the questions that had been bouncing around in his head since the first time he saw *Nick and Nora's Infinite Playlist* and the seeds for his escape were planted.

Along the quiet stretch of empty road, Logan pedaled hard. His heart was pounding, nearly drowning out the sound of his slightly staggered breath. The seven miles home from the restaurant were mostly flat, but he was going faster than usual tonight, energized from his shift instead of exhausted. He had spoken to a couple from Manhattan, who lit up when he told them he was starting at Columbia in the fall.

"New York will be a big change from all this natural beauty," was the first comment they made.

Holding back his eye roll, Logan kept his smile on. People didn't tip waiters who rolled their eyes.

"I can't wait to finally see it. What's the best part of the city?" His calm voice hid the pure excitement he'd been feeling ever since that big, blue envelope had arrived in the mail.

Logan's heart sank a bit, however, when the couple launched into a list of the best restaurants, museums and theaters New York had to offer. Things Logan would never be able to afford. People with money had no idea what life was like for those without it.

The couple had tipped well, in the end, and now he was flying through the night with the promise of an endlessly profitable summer. If he could pull in three hundred a night, like tonight, then he might be able to check off a few things on his big list of "New York things to do." Even a hundred a night would get him there. His full ride covered tuition as well as room and board, but the school required all students on scholarships to come with a little money saved. There were ways to get discounted books but for anything outside of school he was on his own.

Really on his own.

He'd have to buy a bike once he got there. It would be too expensive to ship this one, even though he loved it. His first summer job at fifteen had earned him the money for it, and he kept it well maintained. It had been his ticket to freedom back in Helena, and though he'd gotten his license right at sixteen he'd always been more comfortable on his bike.

Most kids at school had gotten cars as graduation presents. He'd gotten a new bike helmet and had been thrilled. His mom had probably gone without something she'd needed that month to be able to offer it to him.

As he turned a corner, the lake loomed into view: a deep, dark spread of nothingness save for the speckles of light along the banks where the houses were lit up. The same houses he spent every afternoon cleaning before his shift at the restaurant.

But tomorrow, he finally had his first day off since starting two weeks ago. He would be able to head to the lake to swim, unaffected by the cold the way the tourists were. He'd go down to Wayfarer Park maybe, jump off the cliffs like when he was a kid. After all, this was technically his last summer of being a kid.

His eyes and mind on the lake, Logan didn't see the car's headlights until they were almost right in front of him.

CASSIE WAS REACHING the limits of her patience and love for her family. She'd been up at the lake for a week now, alone with her dad. And if she had to sit through one more afternoon of fishing or yet another dinner in front of the TV watching the Mariners she would scream.

Not wanting to ruin her family's summer vacation before it had even truly begun, she'd been texting her best friend Marissa all day, trying to convince her to come up for the night. It was a three-hour drive from Helena, but they'd driven longer for less urgent things. And this was pretty urgent.

Finally, around three in the afternoon, Cassie's phone buzzed and she swiped it open eagerly.

"I took tomorrow off," Marissa said, without even a 'hello.' Her voice sounded echoey. "I'm already driving up."

"Awesome!" Cassie's face broke into a smile and she got up out of bed for the first time that day. She had flat out refused to go fishing with her dad that morning, telling him she had cramps. That always got him out of her room in a hurry. "I guess I'll actually have to change out of my pajamas then."

"Nah, stay that way, you look hot," a male voice spoke up.

Cassie's heart sank.

"Spencer's with you?" she whispered. Of course he could still hear her, but Cassie wanted to annoy her boyfriend. Her patience for Spencer had worn off long before summer had started.

Marissa laughed. Spencer said nothing, so Cassie knew it had worked.

"I can't keep him away, sorry," Marissa said, not sounding sorry at all.

Bringing him had probably been Marissa's idea in the first place, since it meant she got to spend a few hours in the car with him. Cassie knew her best friend had always been into Spencer.

It didn't bother Cassie one bit. After those first few weeks of dating when everything Spencer did or said was hilarious and cute, Cassie had been pretty lukewarm towards him, despite his killer looks that had every other girl in school swooning. Now approaching their one year anniversary, Cassie found herself part of a couple who everyone, except her, expected to stay together forever. Cassie hoped that with a little creative plotting this summer, Spencer would somehow fall for Marissa and break up with Cassie...so she wouldn't have to break up with him.

She didn't actually expect the plan to work. This wasn't the first time she'd had a brilliant strategy to push Marissa and Spencer together and finally get rid of him. But every time she worked up the courage to try, her dad would say something to remind her how proud he was that she was dating a Huntington.

"Where do you want to go tonight, Marissa?" Cassie

decided to pretend Spencer wasn't there, as usual, and just talk to Marissa.

"We'll talk when we get up there, Cass, we're wasting precious road trip time that could be spent listening to music." Spencer was the one who responded anyway, and Marissa giggled. Cassie let out a long, slow breath and counted to ten in her head.

"Fine, call me when you get to Finney's Point." That was about twenty minutes away and would give her time to put the finishing touches on whatever outfit she came up with.

"See you soon!" Marissa squealed.

With a slight pang as she ended the call, Cassie wished she was that excited to spend a few hours with Spencer. What had promised to be a fun break from her less-than-stellar start to the summer would now turn into the same old weekend party scene she wanted desperately to break away from, if only she could figure out how.

Still, she was excited to see Marissa, and would put up with Spencer if she had to. At least it would make her dad happy.

Her dad loved Spencer. He was like the perfect mix of sporty ruggedness that her parents surrounded themselves with, plus the added advantage that his insanely wealthy parents were members of the best country club in the state. Apparently belonging to the second best club wasn't enough for her parents.

That was at least one good thing about being at the lake for the summer: No country club. And now, after a pretty chill week, things were finally about to get interesting.

Her dad had been the one to suggest an extra-long trip to their lake house this summer in order to spend time together as a family before she left for school. But he'd been grouchy and tense ever since they'd arrived, and her mom still hadn't come up yet, too busy with a big charity event she was planning. Her older sister Diana would be here at some point but she didn't know when. Everyone was busy this summer except her.

Cassie would just have to do what she'd always done and make do with what she had. To be fair, it wasn't a bad life, not even close, and most of the time she was happy. She'd focus on her Marissa/Spencer plan tonight, and that would make her even happier.

EIGHT HOURS LATER, however, Cassie was back to hating everyone and everything. Spencer was drunk, and kept trying to reach under her skirt as she drove.

"Stop it!" she hissed for the fifteenth time since they'd left the bar. The bouncer hadn't even looked at their fake IDs once they'd seen Spencer's. He used his older brother's, and the Huntington name was enough to get them in anywhere, thanks to daddy owning half the properties out here. "Marissa is right there."

Spencer sniggered and looked in the backseat.

"She's passed out! She won't even know..." He slid his hand up her thigh again, and leaned across to nuzzle her neck.

"I need to concentrate, you asshole." Cassie didn't even try to sound cute. She was pissed.

She turned to shove him back into his seat, and punched his arm for good measure. He laughed hysterically, and she rolled her eyes before turning them back on the road. She opened her mouth to insult him again, but instead, a loud gasp escaped her lips.

A bike was headed straight for the car.

CHAPTER TWO

LOGAN SKIDDED off the road with a jerk of the handlebars and bumped along the rocky edge until the bike slid out from under him. When he slammed into the ground, there was a distinct "pop" as his shoulder hit hard. A string of curses burst from his mouth as he rolled to his other side.

From the road, there was the sound of the car zooming by, and he tried to pull up his head enough to get a good look at it. The night was too dark; all he saw was that it was a tiny little something, and maybe red.

But it was hard to tell, since his entire field of vision was red with pain. The pop in his shoulder was now a dull throbbing and he couldn't move it very well. He turned onto his back, staring up at the sky, vaguely aware of how pretty it looked all littered with stars. Standing was out of the question for the moment, so he just looked at the distant twinkling spots instead.

It was entirely possible the twinkling spots were not actually there and he'd hit his head harder than he realized. The shock was still pulsing through him and his mind decided to focus on anything other than what had happened. In a few months he wouldn't even be able to see the stars—the actual stars. He couldn't imagine what that was like.

Logan's breath was coming out in short bursts, his chest tight as his muscles tensed in reaction to the pain. He closed his eyes, trying to get his breathing under control. Long deep inhales, slow smooth exhales.

It worked for a few minutes and he alternated calm breathing and staring up at the night sky. But the throbbing was getting worse, and Logan knew he couldn't lay on the ground forever. He considered his options.

He could call his cousin, Hideki. But Logan was pretty sure he was still at his job working late at the pizza place two towns over.

Who else could he call? With a groan, he remembered his aunt and uncle were out of town.

The one time they're away all summer, and of course something like this happens.

Logan felt for his jacket pocket with a shaky hand, and unzipped it to grab his phone, thanking his lucky stars twinkling above it hadn't broken in the fall. He sent a text to Hideki anyway, just in case.

You done with work? I kinda had an accident.

Logan looked over at his bike and let out a sigh of relief. It looked fine. The tightness in his chest loosened a bit. He really didn't want to spend his first paycheck of the summer repairing it. His shoulder twinged and he grimaced. He'd probably have to use it on repairing himself, instead.

His phone pinged.

Oh, that sucks. Work's done but at a party in Lakeside. Where are you?

Logan cursed again. All the way on the other side of the lake. It would take him just as long to walk home as it would to wait for a ride. He was only two miles away. On his bike, it would take him less than ten minutes. Walking would be slow and painful, but he could manage. Probably.

No worries, Logan replied. ***I think I can make it home. I'm not far.***

He sighed and put his phone back in his pocket. He was still lying on the ground, staring up at the stars. The silence was calming, but he didn't want to fall asleep out here. Shaking his head, he slowly pushed himself up to a sitting position. Then, even slower, he held his arm close to his body to steady his shoulder then heaved himself into a standing position.

A hot streak of fire ripped through his shoulder. He pushed at it with trembling fingers, hoping he wouldn't feel a bone poking out of the skin or anything. It didn't feel like a broken bone. Not that he'd ever had one, but the pop he'd heard was worrying. Dislocated maybe? There was a lump around his shoulder joint and Logan let out yet another slew of profanities into the dark night.

He plopped back onto the ground, feeling a bit lightheaded all of the sudden. A quick search online revealed popping his shoulder back into place was probably not something he should do alone on the side of the road. But once he got home, his cousin would definitely be up for it. They'd gotten into their fair share of scrapes they'd wanted to hide from their parents over the years, and Logan knew Hideki would do whatever he could to help him. In the meantime, Logan gently unzipped his jacket and let it slide off his arms. Taking a deep breath, he reached behind him to get it, trying not to move his right arm. After tying the sleeves together, he looped it around his neck and slipped his arm in the opening.

It was probably the ugliest sling in the world, but it would have to do for the next two miles. He didn't usually listen to music while riding home, but he decided he would need the extra motivation and put his headphones in. Looking for the perfect song took a bit of time, and he could only stall the inevitable painful walk home for so long. With the music turned up, he was finally ready to get started. Just as he bent to pick up his bike, a flash of red caught his eye and he turned his head. A car was pulling up on the other side of the road.

It was the first car he had seen since the small and possibly red one had run him off the road. Eleven at night wasn't exactly rush hour. He still took precautions at night, not that it had helped him tonight. His bright yellow jacket and lights all over the bike would have made him visible from a good half mile away. It hadn't done him any good earlier, but maybe whoever had noticed him now would offer him a ride home.

His heart sank when he saw it was a brand new Mercedes SUV with vanity plates reading HART<3. With a sigh, he turned off his music, ignoring every bone in his body urging him to run in the opposite direction.

Cassie Hart was the last person in the world he wanted to see right now.

The car door opened slowly, and a blond head popped out, her hair shimmering in the moonlight. Cassie stepped out of the car but didn't move closer, instead squinting at him from across the road.

"Are you okay?" she yelled, cupping her hands around her mouth. The cool night breeze whipped her hair around her face, and she pulled it back with both hands.

"Fine!" he yelled back and turned to pick up his bike. He let out a sharp gasp as his body shifted forward. Tears appeared in the corners of his eyes, but he blinked them away. No way was he going to let Cassie Hart see him cry.

He heard her running across the road but didn't turn to look at her. Getting his bike upright without screaming in pain was taking all of his concentration. Could he push it along with only one arm? Hopefully.

"What happened?" Her voice was so close, she must have been right behind him. He still didn't turn around, though.

"Nothing. Just some crazy driver ran me off the road." The rough and angry voice that burst from his mouth was barely recognizable as his own.

Cassie inhaled sharply. "You're hurt."

"Nice powers of observation." He rolled his eyes, though she couldn't see it.

Logan knew he was being mean, but Cassie had been mean, too, for the past 6 years. Well, not mean to him, exactly. Their last names of Hanes and Hart meant they'd been sitting next to each other in homeroom since middle school. She'd barely glanced his way their entire lives. Before tonight, he couldn't have been sure she even knew he existed. So no, she'd never been mean to him. That much was true.

But he'd noticed over the years how she would treat people. She'd be chatty and nice one day, and then ignore them the next. She'd gossip about people sitting just a few chairs away, as if they couldn't hear her. Cassie Hart was the typical queen bee, head cheerleader, down to the impossibly beautiful face and body, and crazy rich parents.

And, of course, her crazy rich parents would have a lake house. He'd probably even cleaned it a few times. And she wasn't the only one from Helena Prep that would be up here this summer. The season was just getting started, and by the Fourth of July the lake would be crawling with all the people Logan wanted so desperately to get away from.

But Cassie was the one he really didn't want to see him like this: dirty, smelling like the restaurant, with his arm in a makeshift sling on the side of the road at midnight.

Why'd it have to be her?

"Logan, do you need help?"

At this, the sound of his name, he finally turned to face her, his brows drawn together at the genuine concern in her voice.

She looked perfect. Of course she did. He couldn't help but notice how much of her tanned legs he could see thanks to her short jean skirt, so artfully frayed it must have been expensive. A sequined tank top beneath a luxury brand hoodie completed the casual yet sleek look he saw every day on the people he served at the restaurant. She was a walking, talking reminder of everything he wasn't, and he hated everything about her right now. Even the fact that she was mysteriously being nice to him.

"Why do you want to help me?" he spat, lifting his chin.

She raised an eyebrow, a hand on her hip.

"I realize the impression you probably have of me, but do you really think I'm the kind of person who'd just drive by someone laying on the side of the road?"

It was like a punch to the gut. His head, already fuzzy from the fall and throbbing shoulder, tried to somehow justify his anger towards her.

It was true; he didn't know her. He'd gone to school with her for years, and they'd never spoken a word to each other before tonight. Had that been entirely because of her? Or was he partly to blame?

"Well, thanks, but I'll be fine." He didn't have the time or energy to deal with the fact that he was probably the one being a jerk right now. Nearly getting run over had to give him some sort of pass for things like that.

As he turned and walked away, he could hear a slight huff of frustration from her. He smiled, despite everything, thinking that he'd actually said no to a cheerleader who wanted to give him something.

He just didn't think she had anything he really wanted.

CHAPTER THREE

WELL THAT WENT WELL.

Cassie watched Logan walk away, guiding his bike with one hand, the other strapped oddly to his chest with his jacket. At least the night was warmer than usual. The really cold nights weren't until later in the summer. This was still the golden period of warm summer nights and the lake was a perfect cool break from the hot days.

Cassie felt like running into the lake now to cool off her burning face.

Logan had been so mean to her, and she just wanted to help.

This is what you get for trying to be a good person, she told herself, *when you are clearly a horrible one.*

What she'd told him wasn't true. She *was* the kind of person who'd leave someone on the side of the road. She just had, fifteen minutes ago.

Her heart was beating a mile a minute as she got back into her car. Had he seen her behind the wheel of the red VW bug from earlier? It was Marissa's, and completely impractical for Montana winters, but super fun to drive in the summer. Well, fun until she almost ran someone over with it.

It had been dark, so maybe he hadn't seen her. Everything had gone by so fast, she wasn't even sure it had really happened until she'd come back to see Logan standing there, his arm tied up and his face red with pain.

Now it was her face that was red, with a pain in her gut to match. As she drove home, she tried not to think about how bad it could have been. What would she have done if he'd still been lying on the ground? She walked into her house, distracted by the endless possibilities of how this night could have been even worse, not even noticing that her dad was standing in the kitchen waiting for her until she heard his angry voice.

"Didn't see enough of Spencer earlier, did you?" He stood with a hand on his hip, very similar to the pose she'd just taken with Logan.

Cassie blanched. She wasn't expecting a fight now, though she'd been prepared for one a half hour ago when she'd walked in the door supporting a totally passed out Marissa. Cassie had left her best friend snoring in the guest bedroom, putting a glass of water and empty trash can within arm's reach before running out again to check on Logan.

Now she was caught totally off guard. Should she tell her dad what she'd done? He always knew if she was lying. It was like his superpower. Now she almost wished she'd taken up Spencer on his offer to crash at his place. She would have had all night to think up a story.

"Cass, come inside for a few minutes," Spencer drawled when she drove up to his house. He gave her his best puppy eyes, which had worked on her at the beginning of the school year, but she was pretty much immune to them at this point.

She really had to figure out how to break up with him. The drunken dancing with Marissa had apparently done nothing useful besides increase Marissa's crush. Spencer had ignored her completely any time Cassie was nearby.

"I can't leave Marissa here," Cassie said, turning away from his pleading eyes. She looked into the back seat where her best friend was snoring, her skirt hiked up to reveal a thong underneath. Cassie sighed and unzipped her hoodie to put on top of her. Cassie knew Marissa would be embarrassed as hell to know Spencer had seen her like this.

"Bring her in, she can sleep on the couch." His words were a bit slurred and about three volume levels too high for the quiet night. Cassie knew his parents didn't really care, but her dad would. Huntington or not, she was not supposed to be out at all hours with a guy.

"No, I'm really tired. I just want to go home."

"Fi-ine," Spencer drawled, leaning in to kiss her. She turned her head so he got her cheek. When he grunted in protest, she gave him a look she knew he wouldn't remember in the morning. Hopefully he wouldn't remember most of the drive.

"You stink." She wrinkled her nose and shook her head. "Like cigarettes and beer. No thank you. Call me tomorrow when you're sober and showered, please."

With that, she pushed him gently away and closed the car door before he could say or do anything else.

She gagged at the memory of his smoky, stale breath.

The gag made her dad take his hand off his hip and point a finger at her, his eyes hard.

"Don't tell me you drove drunk!"

"No!" she cried, trying to regain control of her emotions. She stalked into the kitchen to get a glass of water, buying herself a little more time. Her dad followed her and leaned again the counter, waiting. It was a routine they had been through before.

Just tell him. He'll know what to do.

"I didn't drink anything tonight."

Her dad raised an eyebrow from across the kitchen.

"I didn't! I don't want college to be like high school. Really."

He pursed his lips but nodded. There'd been a huge lecture at the beginning of the summer after her particularly raucous grad night party. She was supposed to be done with all of the 'high school nonsense' as her parents called it, and it was time to get ready for the real world.

"Where were you?"

"I..." Tears started to form in the corners of her eyes. The heaviness in her stomach was still there, and now her chest was tightening. Her father's eyes bore into hers, demanding answers she didn't want to give. They reminded her of Logan's, so hard and cold with anger, and she covered her face with her hands, reliving that awful moment when she'd lied to Logan's face about what she'd done to him.

Before she knew it, she was blubbering and running into her father's arms. He grunted in surprise at the fierceness of her hug.

"Hey," he said softly, brushing a hand along her hair the way he used to when she was a little girl. "It's okay sweetheart. Whatever it is, I can fix it."

She sniffed and wiped a hand across her eyes, her heart lifting a bit at the familiar words. He was in construction, after all. He was pretty good at fixing things. Taking a deep breath, she launched into the story, the words coming out in a jumble.

"Spencer was distracting me when I was driving us all home in Marissa's car and I didn't see a biker on the road." She felt her dad's arms tense around her, and the gentle patting of her head stopped. Cassie's voice cracked in her rush to explain. "He just fe-fell down! I didn't know what to do, so I-I just kept driving."

Cassie shuddered as she thought about how fast it had all happened. She remembered swerving off the road and bumping along the edge. Spencer had laughed hysterically as she jerked the wheel back and the car found the road again. He told her to turn back and 'scare Hanes again' but she'd barely heard him over her pounding heart. Marissa had jolted awake, mumbling something about Beyoncé, then fell right back down in the seat.

Her dad pulled back and held Cassie by her shoulders, looking straight into her eyes.

"Did you go back to check?" His tone was serious and impenetrable.

Cassie shivered and nodded.

Her dad's eyes grew cold, his lips pursed again in the thinnest of lines.

"Why would you do that?" He dropped his hands from her shoulders, and stalked over to the other side of the kitchen. He ran a hand through his thinning hair.

It was like a rock had rammed into her stomach.

"Why would I go check to see if someone I hurt was okay?" She said the words slowly, trying to figure out why this would be a bad thing.

Her dad turned and looked at her, eyes wide.

"Please tell me the biker didn't recognize you as the driver." His hands gripped the side of the counter.

"I don't think so." She bit her lip. "I dropped off Spencer and Marissa and took my car back out there. Logan was walking, so I don't think he was that hurt. But his arm was all wrapped up."

"Logan? You know the boy?" His voice was urgent and trembling now, knuckles white on the edge of the counter.

Cassie nodded slowly, but her heart was pounding fast now. *Why would that make a difference?*

"From school. We sat next to each other in homeroom. Logan Hanes." Though Cassie was embarrassed to admit that if Spencer hadn't recognized him, she never would have.

Her father's eyes nearly popped out of his head. He threw his hands up in the air and groaned.

"Of course it's the Hanes. Those money grubbing scum will come looking for a check before we can blink." He rubbed his face with his hands. "What did you have to give him?"

"What did I...?" Cassie shook her head, words escaping her as she processed her dad's reaction. It was so far from the comforting 'fix-it' approach she'd been expecting, she was struggling to calm her whiplashed heart.

She'd never heard him talk about anyone like that, even his worst clients. And how did he know Logan, too? How did everyone know Logan except her?

"He didn't want anything. He walked away."

Her father shook his head.

"That's because he didn't know it was you that nearly ran him over." His eyes narrowed, and she felt the rock in her stomach start to roll around. It was his worst 'I mean business' expression. The one she'd seen him give countless guys on his building sites when they tried to explain why a delivery was late or why something hadn't passed inspection. Those guys didn't tend to stick around very long after their mistakes. At least he couldn't fire his daughter.

Right?

"Why should who I am make a difference?" Cassie's head was spinning. She leaned against the counter, exhausted, just wanting this awful night to be over. "I did what I could to help, he said no. It's over, right?'

"You have to find a way to help him." Her dad started to pace around the kitchen. "Check in on him. But don't make it look like it's because you feel responsible. Just friendly."

Cassie let out her breath in a huff. It was like her dad hadn't even heard her!

"I tried. He said he didn't need help."

"Don't take no for an answer!" His voice rose and he turned to point a finger at her again.

She jerked her head back, startled, and crossed her arms over her chest. She felt the edge of the counter dig into her back as she stared wide-eyed at her father glaring down at her. Tears started to pool in her eyes again and she let out a choked sob.

At the sound, her dad took a deep breath and closed his eyes. Crying usually worked to get him to calm down, though it was rare that the tears were actually real.

"Just…figure out a way to make sure that he gets whatever he needs this summer," he said, his voice finally the familiar soft and soothing tone she was used to in crisis situations. "If he was on a bike, he obviously doesn't have a car. Drive him to doctor's appointments. If you see him at the lake, say 'hi'. Invite him to parties, whatever. Just make sure he ends up thinking you're a great girl. So he'll never even think it could possibly have been you."

She bit her lip. This didn't make any sense. She got why it would be bad for anyone to know the accident was her fault. But why was helping some random kid so important to her dad?

Well, not completely random. She did know him, in a way. Not that she'd ever really paid attention to him in school, but that wasn't her fault. They ran in totally different crowds. She couldn't be expected to know everyone. But her dad apparently knew him. And he hadn't seemed to care so much about the accident until he found out it was Logan.

"Is everything okay, Dad?" Her voice was quiet.

"Of course, why?" His gruffness surprised her, yet again. It was late, and she was tired, and every little reaction from him seemed to be amplified a hundred times. She tried so hard to make her parents happy and proud, and ninety-five percent of the time, she did. This was definitely one of those five percent times.

"You just seem…I dunno, tenser than usual." Cassie wanted

to go over and give him a hug, like when she was a little girl, but his rigid back as he paced put her off the idea.

He frowned and crossed his arms, leaning back against the counter again.

"I have a lot on my mind." A deep sigh rumbled through his whole body. "At work."

Cassie decided not to point out that he hadn't been to any job sites or to the office for the past two weeks. But maybe he was working in the office in the house and she just hadn't noticed. He couldn't just be fishing and watching baseball all the time, could he?

"I guess I'll try again with Logan," Cassie said with a shrug and a sigh.

"Thank you, Cass," her dad said with a tiny smile. "It would help me out a lot if you kept the Hanes boy happy this summer. It would be one less thing for me to worry about."

Her smile back was a little confused, but she felt better at how relieved her dad looked. With a sigh, she resigned herself to another encounter with the boy who clearly wanted nothing to do with her. You'd think he'd be happy that the most popular girl in school wanted to help him. But then again, high school was over. She was no longer the most popular of anything. It was a thought that was both freeing and terrifying.

She hugged her dad goodnight and headed off to her room down the hall, thinking it over. She didn't have a clue why it was so important to her dad, but there might be a way that helping him—and Logan—could fit into her summer plans, too. Spencer would hear about her hanging out with someone else and maybe that would be enough to get him interested in Marissa.

Her parents wouldn't be too happy about it, but did they really expect her to stay with him through college? The path her parents had picked for her was a good one, but she wasn't sure it was what she wanted. Parts of it were great. But not all of it. Definitely not the Spencer part.

Going to Columbia had been pretty much a guarantee for her since birth. Both of her parents were alumni and kept up their contacts there. Her grades in high school had been good—better than she'd ever let on to her friends. It's not that she'd intentionally spent four years cultivating a ditzy and gossipy cheerleader attitude in order to fool everyone, it was more that it was what people expected of her, so she played into it. It was easier to just let everyone think what they wanted about her. Except her teachers, who she'd been sure to impress as often as possible, and who had consequently written stellar recommendations for her.

Now she had acceptance letters to three different schools: Harvard, Stanford, and Columbia. Her parents obviously wanted her to go to New York, but when she'd hesitated, they'd sent checks to all three, holding her spots. Now she just had to choose.

They'd been to visit all three over winter break. The snow in the east didn't scare her one bit, but the distance would be hard. In the back of her mind, she thought she'd go to UM Missoula with Marissa. She got accepted there, too, as a backup, but once the Columbia letter had arrived, her parents wouldn't let her consider anything but Ivy League.

Cassie sighed as she climbed into bed. She'd just agreed to yet another thing her dad wanted her to do. She was tired of living the life her parents planned for her, but also...it was kind of nice. Not having to make these kinds of choices on her own. Her independent streak wasn't *that* big. Life was good for Cassie Hart, and always would be, if she just listened to her dad. He hadn't steered her wrong yet, had he?

So if he wanted her to befriend and help out Logan this summer, then that's what she'd do.

CHAPTER FOUR

LOGAN MADE sure he was out of Cassie's line of sight before he called Hideki.

"Dude, I can't do it. Can you come and get me?"

Logan hated to admit that he needed help, and especially hated pulling his cousin out of a party (a good one, by the background sounds Logan could hear on the phone), but he'd have done the same in a heartbeat for Hideki.

Both only children, the two cousins had considered each other as brothers since they were little and had alternated spending the summer at each other's houses. Logan had always preferred the summers he was at the lake more than when Hideki was in Helena. The past three years he'd been able to convince his mom he could make more money over the summer at the lake, and she relented. He did miss his mom, though, when he was away, and he didn't like thinking of her spending so many nights all alone in their apartment. His dad had been out of the picture for years and it had been just the two of them for as long as he could remember.

Aunt Caroline assured Logan that it was good for his mom to have a little time for herself. Besides, everyone knew that

Caroline was the better cook. She'd met her husband while living in Japan for a few years after college and she had learned to cook all the best dishes, and then combined them with Midwestern staples. His three months at the lake every summer were heaven for Logan. Luckily between the manual labor of his various summer jobs and the bike riding, he kept in pretty good shape.

Not in good enough shape to avoid this injury, he thought miserably as he saw his cousin's beat up Ford F-150 pull onto the side of the road.

Logan looked behind him to be sure Cassie hadn't followed him, and started to lift his bike into the truck bed.

"Woah, let me help you," Hideki called out the open window, rushing to open his door. Shaking his head, he ran around to the back. "I didn't realize you were seriously hurt."

"It's not serious," mumbled Logan, as he watched his cousin lift the bike effortlessly with his two working shoulders. "Just a dislocated shoulder. I think."

"I should take you to the hospital then."

Logan shook his head.

"Absolutely not." He bit his lip. It wasn't like his mom's family didn't know she had money trouble. After all, they were the ones hosting Logan every summer so that his mom could work longer hours. But Logan didn't know if she'd told them she'd lost her job recently. No, not lost—left. Logan's mom had been very specific with her words when she'd told him right after graduation a few weeks ago.

"Fine, no hospital. Dr. Google, then?" Hideki grinned.

"Way ahead of you." Logan made his way to the passenger side and climbed in. Hideki took his seat again behind the wheel and they drove off.

"Not to be an ass when you're in pain, but this was not on the BSE list, man," Hideki said with a shake of his head.

"I didn't do it on purpose," grumbled Logan.

They'd promised each other this would be the 'Best Summer Ever' at the lake before they both left for college. They'd even made a list. It wasn't a complicated one: as many parties, as many girls, and as much money as possible. There were favorite spots and traditions on the list, too, but Hideki was right that getting seriously hurt was not on there.

It stung a little how close Logan had been to home. In less than five minutes, they were at his aunt and uncle's bungalow. It was small compared to the other houses in the area—he'd cleaned places that could fit their whole house into its foyer. But for someone who'd only ever lived in tiny two-bedroom apartments, it always felt like a palace when he visited. He used to share a bedroom with Hideki but this summer their schedules were so off, they'd be waking each other up all the time that way. So Logan was camped out in the office.

Tonight, however, he didn't hesitate to head straight to Hideki's room.

"I need to lay down on something high and flat," he started. He sat down on his cousin's bed and pulled out his phone to show him the video outlining the steps they'd need to take to put his shoulder back in place.

Hideki's eyes grew wide.

"I know we've done some stupid stuff, but I don't know if I can do that. What if I mess up your shoulder?"

"It's already messed up!" Logan cried, and grimaced at the bolt of pain his sudden jerky movements sent through his shoulder. "You just need to help me tie something to my arm to weigh it down."

After a bit more argument, and two more viewings of the video, Logan managed to convince Hideki that this would work. They set up in the kitchen, where the table was high enough he could lie on his stomach and let his arm hang over the side.

Nearly delirious from pain and exhaustion at this point, Logan tried not to think too hard about what he was about to do as Hideki strapped a small barbell to his wrist with an ace bandage. Aunt Caroline would flip if she knew they were planning to use her antique table as a substitute for a hospital bed...again.

This was probably the most serious injury they'd had to handle on their own; however. Thank goodness all Logan had planned for his day off was relaxing at the lake. Even if this worked, he'd be in no shape to do anything else the next day.

The minutes dragged on as Logan waited for the weight attached to his wrist to slowly move his shoulder back in place. It had seemed the safest of the different techniques he'd found to help a dislocated shoulder, but it was the longest. And possibly the most painful.

"So, how'd this happen?" Hideki asked, his eyes never leaving Logan's face as it twisted in agony. Logan was 99% sure he'd pass out from the pain. Or throw up. Hideki did not like seeing anyone throw up.

That was a big reason why until this 'best summer ever,' they'd never gone to any crazy parties. Sneaking a beer or two from the fridge when his parents were away was about the worst they'd ever done. Nowhere near barfing point.

"Some jerk ran me off the road," Logan said through gritted teeth. "Probably drunk. I was lit up like a Christmas tree in my jacket. No way they couldn't see me."

Logan grunted and shifted a little on the table. In the rush to get started, they'd forgotten pillows to cushion the hard wood against his face. It was too late to mention it now. He'd handled so much pain already tonight, he could deal with laying on a flat surface for a few more minutes.

"He didn't stop?" Hideki's eyebrows shot up.

Logan attempted to shake his head against the table. That

hurt and made the room start to spin. He closed his eyes and took a deep breath. The talking was helping distract him from the pain.

"No. And to make matters worse, Cassie Hart drove by in her big-ass fancy truck and asked if I needed help."

"Who's Cassie Hart?"

"She's this girl from school…" He trailed off, not sure how to explain. The town here was so small, they didn't really have cliques. They barely had a basketball team.

"She's a cheerleader," said Logan, finally. That should be a pretty universally understood stereotype, one that Cassie fit to a T.

"Why would it be worse to have a hot cheerleader stop to help?" Hideki's eyebrows were now scrunched in confusion.

"I didn't say she was hot!" Logan turned to glare at his cousin, but liquid fire shot through his shoulder and neck. He turned back to glare at the floor.

"Duh, cheerleaders are always hot." Logan didn't have to see him to know he was rolling his eyes.

"She's this super popular—and fine, hot—cheerleader, who's never spoken to me before despite sitting next to me for six years in homeroom. And tonight, of all nights, she sees me like this." He gestures with his good arm down at his torn and dirty clothes, his arm hanging loosely by his side. "She kept asking if she could help me."

"And you said?"

"Of course not! I don't need her help! I can handle it on my own."

Logan shifted again on the table and cringed. Okay, maybe he couldn't handle it entirely on his own. But he didn't need someone like Cassie to help him, that's for sure.

"Just so I'm clear," Hideki said, his eyes never leaving

Logan's face. "A hot rich girl stopped to help you and you said no?"

"I didn't say she was rich, either."

Another eye roll that was practically audible.

"Super popular, drives a 'big-ass fancy truck' and up here in the summer from Helena? Totally rich."

Logan bit his tongue. Compared to him and his mom, everyone was rich. He was crazy jealous of Hideki and everything he had, while his cousin spent his time wishing he lived in one of the big houses by the lake. It was all so dumb. He couldn't wait to get away to school, where no one knew him and no one knew he came from nothing. New York would be where he could make the life he wanted for himself. It would be so much better. It had to be.

With a sudden shift, Logan's shoulder seemed to lock back into place. The throbbing had dulled slightly, and the tightness in his chest loosened.

"Hey, I think that's it," he said, sitting up slowly. He reached over to slide off the weight. When he gingerly touched his shoulder, he smiled, relief crashing over him. "Looks like it worked."

No expensive hospital trip needed.

Hideki looked half relieved, half worried.

"Great! But will you still head to the doctor tomorrow to check it out?"

Logan groaned and swung his legs over the side of the table.

"I thought all the nagging adults were away for the weekend."

Hideki shoved him on his uninjured side.

"You have the whole summer at the restaurant and cleaning houses. You don't want to miss any shifts because you can't lift things."

"It'll be fine," Logan said, hopping off the table. "I'll ice it right after I shower. Thanks for your help, man."

Hideki looked him up and down, his brows drawn together.

"Do you...need any help in the shower?"

Logan laughed. Hideki's puckered face let Logan know he really wanted the answer to be no.

"I think I can manage it. Thanks."

He raised his right hand for a high five that Hideki took a good ten seconds to return. Logan didn't lower his arm while he waited, needing to show his cousin that he'd be okay. When he finally got the halfhearted slap against his palm, he smiled and headed off to the bathroom, alone at last.

CHAPTER FIVE

AN INCESSANT BUZZING from her phone woke Cassie up the next morning. Swiping sleepily at the screen, she found a text message from her mom waiting.

Sorry I won't make it up there until next week. This charity thing is crazy. I swear they just can't handle anything without me. Hope you're having fun with your dad.

A frown line appeared between Cassie's perfectly groomed eyebrows. The whole reason she'd been dragged to the lake this summer was for family bonding time, but all three of them had only been together the first night. Her mom had gone back the very next day, citing issues with the charity event. Cassie knew the event was important to her mom, but this was getting a little ridiculous.

Since marrying her dad right after college, her mom had never had to work. Instead, she had a 50-hour per week schedule of events and committee meetings and galas that Cassie could barely keep track of. But her mom seemed to be even busier than usual lately, not to mention distracted. Her parents had never been the super gushy romantic type, but the one night they'd all been at the lake house had felt off, somehow. There was something buzzing at the back of Cassie's head about her mom working more being somehow related to her dad suddenly working less...

But she was too tired to think about it that hard right now.

At least they'd all be together once her sister Diana came up for the Fourth of July week. Her summer internship at a law firm in Helena kept her busier than both of her parents, but that week was a nonnegotiable. It always had been, ever since they'd been little. Their parents both took off the entire week, no exceptions. The party they threw was one of the highlights of the summer for their friends.

Cassie didn't care as much about the party as she did about finally having her big sister in the house. She had so much to talk to her about. What college should she choose? Why were their parents being super weird all of the sudden? And Cassie's biggest concern she hoped her big sister could solve—how could she break up with Spencer without actually having to do it herself, thereby crushing her parents' dream of a Huntington-Hart alliance? Her sister had broken nearly every heart there was at Helena Prep before she had gone off to school in California, their parents included.

California. It was a happy daydream in the dreariness of Montana winters. Cassie had grown up hearing from everyone how beautiful Montana was, but California was something else entirely. When she'd been out to visit her sister at Stanford a few times, everything seemed lighter and brighter. The air even felt sunnier. But her parents were anxious for at least one of their daughters to go to Columbia. Yet something deep inside Cassie wanted to rebel and follow in her big sister's footsteps. Di had done so well out there. Maybe Stanford would be the right place for Cassie, too?

Groaning at the flurry of thoughts swirling around in her head before 8 a.m., Cassie flopped back down on her bed and covered her head with a pillow. She didn't want to think about college, not yet. There was still the whole summer to worry about that. Well, maybe not the whole summer. Her dad would need to send a final check somewhere before September.

Her phone buzzed again and she nearly cried. She needed at least another few hours of sleep, but the world seemed against her getting any at all.

Hey are you up?

It was Marissa. Before she could think too hard about the decision, Cassie dragged herself out of bed, stumbled out the door and made her way down the hall to the guest bedroom. Her eyes were barely open, but she knew the hallway here with her eyes closed. And much better than the hallway at her house in Helena, where her mother insisted on redecorating every few months. At home, Cassie was always running into a new table or painting when she would try to sneak back into her bedroom at night.

Here at the lake house, nothing much had changed since she was little. They'd updated the kitchen and bathrooms ten years ago, but it was still the same cozy rustic wood interior and antlered decoration that she'd grown up with. The hall was and had always been mercifully free of random items for her to run into. The massive windows on one side looked out onto the cool, blue depths of the lake, but Cassie barely noticed it this morning with her eyes only half open.

At the doorway to Marissa's room, Cassie paused and rubbed her sleepy eyes. Seeing an equally bleary-eyed Marissa still laying flat on the bed, curled on her side with her phone in her hand, Cassie crawled wordlessly under the covers next to her and shut her eyes.

"Sorry I was so wasted last night," Marissa mumbled, her

fingers tapping away. "And thanks for not posting any photos of me passed out online."

"Shhh, still sleeping."

"Did I do anything too stupid?"

"Yes, you danced *Coyote Ugly* style at the bar."

"Shut up!" Marissa giggled, turning over to shove Cassie, who kept her eyes firmly shut. She considered telling her about all the dancing she'd actually done with Spencer but was too exhausted to work on her master plan. She had all summer to get the two of them together.

"Just go back to sleep, I'm exhausted."

"We didn't stay out *that* late, did we?"

Cassie kept her mouth shut as tightly as her eyes. She didn't want to admit to Marissa that she'd gone out again after dropping her off. And then there was the long and weird conversation with her dad, who was suddenly very interested in 'the Hanes boy' as he'd called Logan.

With a sigh, Cassie rolled over and opened her eyes. Now that she was thinking about Logan and the promise she'd made to her dad, there would be no going back to sleep for a long time. She rubbed her eyes again and looked at the smiling and eager face of her best friend next to her in bed, a little pang whipping through her heart. Marissa's dark curls were cute even when they were messy. They were physically total opposites, yet so alike in personality. Cassie would really miss her in the fall. Though she might not know if she'd be East Coast or West Coast, she hadn't yet found a way to let Marissa know she was most definitely not going to Missoula with her.

One secret at a time.

"No, it wasn't that late," Cassie said with a smile, turning on her side to face Marissa. "And we're up early enough to grab some breakfast at The Ranch."

Marissa's eyes lit up.

"Should we text Spencer to see if he wants to come?"

Ignoring the lump forming in her stomach at her friend's excitement, Cassie shook her head firmly.

"Just girls today."

Marissa beamed, her crush on her best friend's boyfriend apparently not so strong as to warrant giving up a girls-only brunch. Cassie's wide smile of relief was brief.

She really did need to break up with him soon.

IN THE END it wasn't Spencer that interrupted their brunch. Marissa's mom called her halfway through and demanded she come home early. Despite Marissa's best and most creative pleading, it was apparently not negotiable. They headed back to the house so she could drop off Cassie and get her things.

"This is total crap," Marissa said, shoving her clothes from the night before into her bag. "I'll be back next week, I promise. I'm only working two days."

"I'll be fine," said Cassie, waving a hand. "I'll be here, busy not working."

Marissa stuck her tongue out at her and Cassie threw a pillow in her direction. They both laughed, but the lump from earlier was back in her stomach. Cassie didn't really want to be alone all day, with her mood now wildly different than it had been at the same time just twenty-four hours earlier.

Instead of bored, she was anxious. She'd been counting on Marissa to distract her from what she had to do. All it took was a few texts from Spencer, however, (**Hey babe, so it looks like my ride just left early. Wanna pick me up and have some fun today?**) to motivate her to get in touch with Logan somehow. If she couldn't work her 'Marissa is great' angle anymore, she could at least get started on the 'Cassie is busy with someone else' part of her plan. Knowing it wouldn't be that easy, Cassie hoped that if she brushed him off enough, Spencer would eventually get the idea she wasn't interested anymore.

This whole request from her dad still bugged her, though. Why was it so important to him that Logan be okay? The thought was swirling around in her head but she had no idea where to begin. How did her dad even know his name?

Cassie grew more and more frustrated as she set about finding Logan on social media. At first it seemed like there was a match: a Logan Hanes was in her incoming freshman group at Columbia. But the profile was totally locked down and the picture was something weird and artsy with sharks so she had no way of knowing if it was even him.

He seemed to have zero information public, and most of his accounts were private so she couldn't even try to glean information that way about where he was staying this summer. Did his family have a place up here? Most people did. Had she seen him previous summers? Honestly, she couldn't remember, and shame prickled at the back of her mind. Twenty-four hours ago, she wouldn't have even been able to place his face, but now he was all she could think about.

All because she'd nearly killed him with her car. Well, Marissa's car. Maybe it was a good thing she'd left early after all. There'd be less chance of Logan spotting the car around town.

After an hour of fruitless searching, Cassie found herself scrolling through Instagram, trying to ignore the gnawing at her stomach at the thought of failing her father. How could she help Logan if she couldn't even find him?

Suddenly, there he was in her feed. Someone had posted a selfie at Chez Pierre, one of the nicer restaurants in the next town over. Logan was standing right behind a blonde, smiling girl, a tray balanced on his arm and a look of concentration on his face. Cassie looked at the comment.

Good food and cute waiters. What else can a girl ask for on her birthday?

She frowned. Who had posted this, anyway? She looked at the name again. Brittney something. Cassie tried to remember who she was. A daughter of one of her dad's business partners, maybe? She followed way too many people to remember how she knew them all. Cassie checked out Brittney's other pictures, and there were two more from the restaurant last night. One of them had Logan in the background, with a similar caption calling him cute.

Cassie frowned and looked at the pictures again.

He was kind of cute, Cassie had to admit, just a little skinnier and nerdier than she usually fell for. Not that big and beefy was really her type either; it was just the type that she always seemed to end up with. She'd never really noticed Logan before, but apparently Brittney whoever had zeroed in on him right away. Was it his deep brown eyes that had grabbed her attention? Or his dark blond hair, worn slightly longer than most guys at school did? It was combed neatly in the pictures, but last night it had been sticking up all over the place like he'd been running his hands through it. His expression had been angry, too, when Cassie had seen him, not the concentrated-yet-light-hearted half smile he of course would need to put on to keep the patrons of the restaurant happy.

He was *really* cute, she realized the more she looked at him. There was even a little dimple on his cheek that was doing something funny to Cassie's stomach the longer she stared at it. Why had she never noticed him? Was she really so shallow that she only noticed jocks?

She shook her head and tossed her phone down on the bed.

She didn't need to think he was cute to help him, though it would certainly help her quite a bit in order to make Spencer jealous. Now that she knew where Logan worked, it would be easy enough to figure out where he was staying this summer, and she could finally get this plan started and her summer back on track.

CHAPTER SIX

"LOGAN! There's a hot girl at the door for you!"

From his seat on the couch in the living room, Logan nearly spit out his soda on his aunt's clean beige rug. He was playing *Call of Duty* with Hideki and was losing, thanks to one arm being mostly immobile. The crushing pain from the previous night was gone now that his shoulder was back in place but it was still plenty sore.

When he jumped up, however, a bolt of pain streaked through him like lightning. He took a deep breath and headed to the door. There was a sinking feeling in his stomach that he knew who it would be, but he had no idea how she'd found him.

"Hi," said Cassie Hart, smiling brightly as if she'd been invited to come over. She was standing there in all her perfect golden blonde glory, like some real life YouTube makeup star. Except her face seemed mostly bare of anything, which made her even prettier somehow.

Not that he noticed or anything.

"Um, hi?" Logan didn't even try to mask the confusion on his face, glad to have it overriding his desire to blush furiously at her unexpected presence on his porch.

"How are you feeling today?" She tilted her head, her mouth turned down in a little pout.

"Um, fine?" He held his arm closer to his chest. The ace bandage they'd used last night to attach the weight was now being used as both a sling and to keep an ice pack strapped to his shoulder. He knew he looked ridiculous, but he hadn't planned on seeing anyone today. With a sudden jolt of panic, he realized he was still in his pajama pants. But at least his shirt was a neutral gray, and not his normal Shark Week matching set his mom had given him for his last birthday.

"It's dislocated, right?" Cassie nodded at his shoulder.

He raised an eyebrow.

"How do you know? Are you a doctor now?"

She rolled her eyes. It was the first authentic reaction he'd seen from her. All the frowning and worry she'd been showing seemed a little overdone. But maybe it was just because all of her seemed fake to him.

"How many dislocated shoulders on football and basketball players do you think I've seen?"

He held in a groan. Her boyfriend, Spencer, played both. He was headed to Gonzaga on a basketball scholarship, not that he needed it. The Huntingtons practically owned Flathead Lake.

"You should probably have a doctor take a look," Cassie said, not giving him a chance to reply.

How could someone be so hot yet so annoying at the same time?

"I got it popped back in just fine." He lifted his chin slightly, and puffed out his chest. He felt a little silly, but he reminded himself that high school was over. He'd never see her again after this summer, and he had a chance to decide how she remembered him. And it wouldn't be as the dork with a busted shoulder.

"You should still have someone check it out." She put a hand on her hip, tossing back her hair. "Come on, I'll drive you."

Well, that was unexpected.

"What?" He blinked, not sure he'd heard her right.

She shrugged.

"I guess I just feel bad that I couldn't help you last night." She glanced down at her feet, shifting a little from side to side. Logan felt the tiniest pebble of guilt settle into his stomach. He *had* been pretty rude.

"Why? It's not like this was your fault."

She brought a hand up to her hair, twisting a golden lock in her hand. The exaggerated pout was on her face again, along with a tinge of red on her cheeks.

"So you still don't want my help?"

"Yes, he does!" called a voice from the living room.

Logan whipped his head around.

"Shut up, Hideki!"

Logan turned back to Cassie, his face hot. He was going to kill his cousin once she was finally gone.

"Why would you want to help me? Don't you have like, keg parties to go to?"

She rolled her eyes again, waving her hand.

"I've been doing that for four years straight. I'm ready for a break before it starts again in the fall."

"And driving me to a doctor's appointment is your idea of fun?"

"Logan, seriously, what's the issue here?" Hideki appeared at his side and slung his arm around Logan's good shoulder. "I have to get to work soon. I can't take you. You can't ride your bike. Let the hot cheerleader drive you to the clinic. BSE man."

Hideki gave Logan an exaggerated wink. Logan shoved him away, as rough as he could without his shoulder screaming in protest. Now his whole body felt hot, not just his face. He had thought the low point of his summer would be Cassie seeing him on the side of the road. Apparently his cousin had other plans.

When Logan finally gathered the courage to look back up at her, he was surprised to see that her face was as red as his. His resistance softened somewhat, to see that a random guy she didn't know calling her hot made her blush, like she hadn't been hearing it her whole life.

This still didn't make any sense, however. Why would she want to spend time doing anything with him? Where was the bitchy cheerleader he had spent six years sitting next to?

"Look, do you want a ride or not?" She put a hand back on her hip. "I do actually have stuff to do today."

Ah, there she was. That bit of normalcy somehow made the decision easier for Logan. Cassie Hart, Queen Bee he could handle. Blushing and shy Cassie made him a little more confused.

"You're not going to take no for an answer, are you?"

She shrugged.

"Just thank your lucky stars it was me who drove by last night and not someone else who would have given up more easily."

THEY RODE IN SILENCE, Cassie turning up the radio too loud for him to attempt conversation. So she wanted to help him, but not talk to him? He didn't have much brain space to worry about that, however, since the closer they got to the clinic, the more worried he was about how he'd pay. The whole reason for the internet video medical consultation was to avoid paying someone to check him out.

But as they hit a bump in the road and a flash of pain shot

through him, he had to admit that Cassie and Hideki were right. He did need someone to see it, or he'd be out of work all summer and be worse off than before. Columbia had financial aid and other resources for low-income students, but they required him to come with some money saved up. Even if he spent a few hundred today, it would be worth it to be able to go to his shift the next day at the restaurant. Though he'd probably have to take on a few extra houses to clean whenever he could the next few weeks to make up the extra money. While the restaurant got him big tips, he liked the calmness of the empty houses a little better. He'd rather clean more than pick up extra shifts at the restaurant.

When they walked into the clinic, Cassie made a beeline for the desk, taking charge like he was a little kid. She gave his name to the receptionist, took a clipboard full of forms and pulled him down to a chair.

Not even fifteen minutes into this adventure, and Logan was already starting to regret he'd accepted her offer of help.

"Full name?" The pen in her manicured hand was poised over the paper expectantly.

"I can fill them out myself."

She looked over the edge of the clipboard, and eyed his makeshift splint, her lips pressed into a thin line of silent scolding.

"Fine." He sighed and leaned back in his chair. "Logan Hanes."

"No middle names?"

He shifted in his seat.

"Cousteau."

She raised an eyebrow, but thankfully said nothing.

"Date of birth?"

"June 26."

"Ha! I'm two months older than you. April 26th."

Logan rolled his eyes.

"So that gives you the right to be bossy?"

She ignored this.

"Address?"

"For the summer or back in Helena?"

"Permanent I guess. Are you just renting with friends this summer?"

Logan cleared his throat.

"I'm staying with my aunt and uncle. That was my cousin you saw earlier."

Logan held his breath, waiting for the comment that always came. The curious stares, the random comments about different countries in Asia people had visited, the rude questions about adoption. He'd heard it all.

"Ok, so what's the address?" was all she said, nothing registering on her face at all. He let out the breath he was holding and gave her the address.

"Insurance number?"

Logan shifted again in his seat.

"Um, just leave that blank for now. I'll take care of it later."

She looked at him over the edge of the clipboard again, her brows furrowed. He tried to ignore how adorable she was with her forehead all scrunched up.

"I'm not an expert or anything, but this could be kind of expensive without insurance."

"I'll have them bill me. It's not a big deal."

She pursed her lips again and tapped the pen against the clipboard. Without a word, she stood up, put the papers down on her chair, and walked up to front desk.

He let out his breath in a huff, and pushed himself out of the chair with one hand.

Could she be any more annoying?

"You can put everything on my card," she was saying as he marched up next to her.

He blanched when he saw her take a sleek black credit card from her bag and hand it to the nurse.

"What are you doing?" He groaned inwardly at how screechy his voice sounded. He cleared his throat and lowered his voice. "You can't just pay for me."

"Why not? Do you have the money?"

He looked down, hot liquid shame spreading through his veins.

"I'll pay you back," he said, still not looking at her.

He heard her take a deep breath.

"Fine."

He peeked up to see that she was biting her lips. Did she not believe that he'd pay her back?

"I'm good for it. I just need to take on a few more shifts." *A lot more shifts.*

"No rush. I don't want you to hurt yourself more by working too hard."

Logan choked back a laugh. What did she know about working too hard?

"I'll be fine. Thanks for the loan."

He turned and made his way back to their seats. Before he sat back down he grabbed the clipboard off her chair to finish up the paperwork. He didn't need any more of her help.

CHAPTER SEVEN

THE CLINIC WAS PRETTY SLOW that day, and a nurse came out almost as soon as Logan had handed in his papers at the front desk. She led him through a door and he'd followed without another word to Cassie.

"All set?" Cassie looked up from her magazine as Logan came out of the door fifteen minutes later. He nodded.

As she took her purse and stood up, the doctor pushed through the door, waving a piece of paper at Logan. Cassie's heart sank. She hoped it wasn't another bill. Her dad had told her to be nice to Logan, not pay for his medical care. Seeing him with his sling and how much pain he was made her feel so guilty, though, she'd have paid whatever it took to make him better. But how would she explain it to her dad? He was the one that got the credit card bill.

"Logan, here's your prescription," the doctor said, handing him the paper. Cassie breathed a sigh of relief. That wouldn't be too expensive. "Remember it's best not to drive or bike for at least four weeks. No heavy lifting. Don't let anyone pull too hard or lean on your arm." The doctor winked at Cassie, clearly assuming she was Logan's girlfriend.

Logan's face turned such a bright pink he hopefully hadn't noticed that Cassie's had done the same.

"So, no bike for four weeks?" Cassie said once they were in the car. She'd been silent on the drive to the clinic, terrified that she'd just blurt out what she'd done to him. Now it seemed she'd be in chatterbox mode to hide her growing guilt. "Can I drop you off anywhere?"

"No, I'm not working today. I was supposed to go swimming for the first time this summer but..." he shrugged, then grimaced. Her heart sank at the pain on his face he was clearly trying to hide.

"I can take you to the pharmacy. Get you your meds."

"Look, Cassie, I appreciate the lift to the doctor's, but I can handle things. You don't have to be driving me around like some charity case."

"You're not! I'm just helping you out. It's a thing for Columbia." She was thinking so fast, it just slipped out. Crap, how would she explain knowing about that without revealing her social media stalking?

"What? You're going to Columbia?"

She nodded. At least it turned out to be the right Logan Hanes in her freshman group.

He groaned and leaned his head back against the seat.

"Great."

Cassie bristled a little at this.

"It's a big school, I'm sure you won't have to put up with me once we're there." She wasn't sure why she was so upset at the idea he didn't like her, but she didn't want to dig too deep into that right now. "For the summer, however, you're stuck with me."

Logan raised an eyebrow, and her heart raced as she grasped for the threads of an idea to pull together.

"My dad's an alum and there's this alumni...match...thing.

But he's really busy this summer. He told me all about it though, wanted me to reach out since we already know each other from school."

She was talking at super speed now, her stomach churning at the spontaneous lie. It was never this hard to make things up for her parents or teachers. Amazingly, he seemed to be following what she was saying, despite the rapid-fire delivery.

"Alumni match? I haven't heard of that." He frowned.

Ignoring how cute he looked when he was confused, Cassie waved her hand, her heart rate slowing somewhat.

"It's a new thing. I'm sure you got a letter or something at home, but you're here for the summer. Call your mom to check."

"No, she has enough to worry—" He stopped short and shifted in his seat. "I mean, she'll let me know if I get anything from them."

Cassie drove a while longer in silence, thinking through the details of this invented alumni summer connection. It was kind of brilliant, actually. A way for her to check in on him without it looking like that's what she was doing. She'd be able to see if he needed more money for the doctor or a ride somewhere. And it was a good excuse for hanging out with him if Spencer asked. And she really hoped Spencer would ask. Soon.

"Why didn't you just say that when you came by this morning?"

Cassie shrugged.

"I was more worried about getting you to the doctor. You looked really bad last night."

He was silent for a minute.

"Thanks for worrying about me."

"Well, Lions look out for each other." Cassie cringed at the sugary sweetness of her voice. She sounded fake even to herself, but she couldn't expect to break a years-long habit in just a few hours. Giving people what they wanted and expected was what she did best, after all.

Logan raised an eyebrow.

"'Lions look out for each other?'"

"Yeah, it's lame, but you gotta get used to it. Welcome to Columbia!" She smiled her perfected cheerleader smile just as she turned into his driveway. He didn't react, just stared out the window, not getting out of the car.

"So what does this whole match thing involve?" he said slowly.

Her heart raced as fast as her mind did, scrambling for something to say. But she'd been in trickier situations before. The rush of competition and pressure was as familiar to her as the shores of the lake. So why was it so much harder to lie to Logan?

"It's just a few check-ins over the summer with an alumnus. To answer your questions about the school, or about New York, whatever."

"You know New York." It was a statement, not a question, and he said it with a sigh behind his words.

"Oh yeah, really well." Cassie was at her chattiest, brightest best. The peppier you were, the less people noticed anything was wrong with what you were saying. "We go maybe once a year, sometimes twice. For Mom and Dad to see friends, and to go shopping. It's fun. You'll like it."

Logan nodded slowly. Cassie held her breath. Could this actually work? It would make her dad happy. And helping Logan would help her feel a little better about what she'd done, too. She'd put in some time with him this summer, and it would be like the accident had never happened. Spencer would get jealous enough to break up with her and turn to Marissa for comfort. Everyone would get what they wanted.

"So you'll be there to answer my questions instead? Or do I need your dad's number or something?"

Cassie shook her head.

"He is so crazy busy this summer, he's barely even up here at the lake," she lied, thinking about the days that went by with no sign of her dad returning to Helena for work. He'd been on the couch when she'd left that afternoon, watching ESPN and eating cereal.

"Could I get your number then?" Logan stumbled a bit over the words.

The little flutter in her stomach caught Cassie by surprise. A guy hadn't asked for her number since freshman year. She knew it wasn't because Logan was into her—he clearly still wasn't a big fan—but it was a nice reminder that she had her whole life ahead of her for guys to be asking for her number. Spencer would be ancient history by the time she got to New York.

"Just add me on messenger," she said, not wanting to appear too available. No sense getting too close, even if they did end up heading to the same school in the fall. She didn't want the constant reminder in her phone of the guy she almost ran over. It was easier to block someone on social media.

"Done," he said, tapping on his phone. He opened the car door, then turned back to look at her and smiled, his dimple making a brief appearance. "Thanks for the ride. I'll talk to you later."

Cassie sucked in a deep breath and let it out slowly as she watched him walk into the house. She could do this. Just hang out with him a few times, tell him stuff about New York, make sure Spencer knew about it, and then be done with it. It wasn't even a sure thing she'd go to Columbia, but Logan didn't need to know that. All he needed to hear was whatever would make him think she was great, just like her dad had asked.

As she pulled out of the driveway, she thought of messaging him that night to meet again the next day. If she could turn on the charm, it might even all be over by the time the Fourth of July party rolled around. She was already thinking about the crazy good food her mom ordered, and the annual tradition of jumping into the lake from the dock with her sister and Marissa, right as the fireworks started.

She was definitely not thinking about how her heart had skipped a beat when Logan had smiled at her.

"I THINK it's time to call your mom," said Hideki when Logan walked in the door. "My mom and dad will be home tomorrow and it's not like you can hide what happened."

"I will, just give me a minute." Heart still thumping a mile a minute, Logan made his way to his bedroom in the office to lie down. He needed to process all of this.

If someone had told him twenty-four hours ago that he'd be showing up in Cassie Hart's messenger inbox, he would never have believed them. Not only that, he was going to see her again, soon, and multiple times.

He closed his eyes, taking the deep slow breaths he had taught himself to use before heading into a test or math club competition. Usually it worked really well.

Today, however, all the breathing in the world wasn't going to do anything. Hideki had followed him in and was now sitting on the office chair, swiveling back and forth and talking loudly.

"So did you talk to her? I saw you sitting out there in the car. She doesn't seem all that bad, for a cheerleader."

Logan opened one eye and looked at his cousin's eager face. He was the easiest person on the planet to read, which had made lying about all the shenanigans they'd gotten into as kids all the more remarkable. One look at his face and Aunt Caroline knew if he was lying.

Logan was a little better at it, thankfully.

"We were just talking, no big deal."

He wasn't sure why he wanted to keep this whole Columbia thing a secret, other than he didn't want to rub it in Hideki's face. They'd always talked as if they'd both go to Missoula together. Hideki had insisted he was happy when Logan told him about Columbia, but his face hadn't been able to hide his disappointment. They'd barely talked about school, focusing all their attention on the BSE list.

"At least you got a real sling now." Hideki was still talking and swiveling. "What did the doctor say?"

Logan bit his lip.

"No driving or biking for 4 weeks. No heavy lifting."

"Are you serious? So you'll need rides to work and everything?" He stopped swiveling in the chair and worry lines appeared on his forehead. "I don't know if our schedules will line up. Can you even clean or wait tables? Do you want to see if you can do something at the boat house instead?"

Hideki was working at one of the lake's many boat rental places during the day and the pizza place at night. For his house cleaning job, Logan usually biked to the first house and someone gave him a ride to the others. It was pretty physical but he hoped there were still things he could do. He really needed both jobs to make enough for the next year. He wasn't even sure why his cousin was also working two jobs, since his parents were actually able to chip in for college stuff.

Logan didn't say any of that, however.

"Let's just see how I do tomorrow. Maybe it won't be so bad."

Hideki let out a long sigh.

"Fine, but call your mom, okay? Getting in serious trouble with the parental units is not on the list, man."

"Oka-ay, Auntie C," Logan teased.

Hideki threw a pillow at him and stalked out.

Logan debated taking a nap first—he hadn't slept that well with a throbbing shoulder—but decided to just get it over with. His mom insisted on calling instead of texting, which normally he didn't mind, but it was always easier to give her bad news via writing.

His heart was pounding as he found her number in his phone. Taking a deep breath and closing his eyes, he pressed the green call button.

"So I got into a little accident with my bike," he said, without bothering to say hello.

"What happened?" His mom sounded panicked. "Do I need to come up?"

A lump formed in the back of his throat. She had finally found a new job the week before and was working extra hours. He knew she couldn't afford to take any time off.

"No, it's fine. Just my shoulder is a little sore, that's all."

"A little sore?" Her tone had switched to incredulous. "Like how your leg was a little sore last summer when you and your cousin dared each other to jump over a bonfire?"

Logan held back a laugh. That had been pretty awesome, until Aunt Caroline had come down to the beach early to pick them up and had gone ballistic. And then had told his mom about the whole thing.

"I went to the doctor and got some meds. I'll be fine."

His mom sucked in a breath.

"Did you have to use your emergency credit card? Let me know, so I can pay it off as soon as it comes in. I don't want you going off to school with debt."

He'd actually purposely buried the credit card in the bottom of his sock drawer, so he wouldn't be tempted to use it this summer. Four years of hard work during high school could be ruined in a few days of reckless spending.

"No it's fine, Cassie spotted me the money." Logan knew his aunt and uncle probably would have taken care of it had they been home, but his mom hated asking them for help beyond what they already did.

"Cassie?" There was an undercurrent of hope in his mom's voice. There had been no time for Logan to have girlfriends in high school. Study partners were as close as he'd gotten, and his mom had always made that as awkward as possible. He loved her, but part of the reason New York was so attractive would be the distance from his mother once he finally entered the dating pool for real.

"Just a girl from school. Cassie Hart."

There was complete and total silence on the other end.

"Mom?" Logan looked down at his phone to make sure he hadn't accidentally hung up.

"Hart as in Jason Hart?" his mom said finally, her voice an odd, flat tone.

Logan suddenly made the connection.

"Oh right. Is that the place you worked last summer? Hart and Preston or whatever?"

"Yes." His mom's voice was tight. Logan tried to remember how long she'd been at the job. It had only been a few months. Ever since she'd been laid off from her long-time hospital administration job right before Logan started middle school, she'd only managed to get temp jobs. It was hard to keep track of all the places she'd worked over the years.

"So is Cassie a friend? You'll be seeing her a lot this summer?" This time his mom didn't sound that hopeful about a new girl in his life. She sounded...angry almost.

"Um, not really. I mean, she's going to Columbia, and her

dad is an alum, so there's some match program that I'm in. We're supposed to meet up this summer, but he's busy so Cassie might do it instead."

"What do you have to do exactly?" The anger was still simmering in her voice. Logan frowned.

"I don't do anything. She's just supposed to like, tell me about New York and what to expect at school and everything."

His mom sighed.

"Does it have to be the Harts?"

Logan's frown deepened. What was happening? Most things about Columbia had his mom even more excited than him.

'There was supposed to be a letter or something from the school. Did anything come for me?"

"No, I don't see anything, but I've just been leaving things for you on your bed. Maybe I can bring everything when I come up for the Fourth of July."

"You'll be able to come?" Now he was the one sounding hopeful.

"I think so." He could hear the smile in her voice. "Things should be settled by then."

"Settled?"

"I mean settled down," she said quickly.

Logan started to ask something else, but his phone beeped, and he pulled it away from his ear to see the messenger icon appear on the side of his screen.

Cassie was already getting in touch?

"Mom, I have to go," he said, burning with curiosity about what the message said. "I'll call you soon, okay?"

After the obligatory 'I love you' from both sides, he ended the call and quickly swiped open Cassie's message, his chest suddenly tight. It had barely been an hour since she'd dropped him off. Had something changed? He looked around his room. He hadn't left something embarrassing in her car, had he?

Just checking to make sure you were able to get the meds.

His chest deflated a bit. She was going to be worse than Aunt Caroline and his mom combined, apparently.

I'll be okay. It's just around the corner. I can walk.

The blinking dots appeared, and hit bit his thumbnail as he waited for her to finish typing her reply.

I can come over to drive you, I don't mind.

He rolled his eyes.

Don't you have a party or something to go to?

Her reply was rapid-fire.

It's 4 in the afternoon. Everyone knows the good ones don't start till at least 9. So you need a ride or not?

What, are you that bored?

The second he hit send, he regretted it. He had been more than a little rude to her already, and she'd done nothing to deserve it except be nice to him. It wasn't her fault she'd been too popular to pay attention to him in high school. Panic flooded through him. He had to remember Columbia. Even if his mom apparently wasn't a fan of the Harts, they were the first of all the important connections he would make while there. He couldn't afford to mess it up. His phone buzzed, and he took a breath before looking at her reply to his unintentional teasing.

You have no idea. ;-)

Logan blinked, staring at the phone, a million replies racing though his head. Unsure of which one would be better, he hesitated to send a reply.

So he didn't send anything. He just set down his phone on the desk and went to find Hideki.

Their game of *Call of Duty* had been interrupted this morning, and they still had to finish. He wasn't about to let Cassie interrupt too much of his life.

CHAPTER NINE

"HEY KIDDO, you up for a site visit?" Cassie's dad poked his head into her room, and she sprang up off her bed in an instant.

"Totally! I'll get my stuff."

"Okay, hurry up. I leave in ten." He shot her a smile and Cassie beamed back at him.

Faced with yet another endless day of tanning on the beach and watching videos online, Cassie bustled around getting ready, thrilled for more than one reason at her dad's unexpected invitation.

Mostly importantly, it meant that she had a reason not to see Spencer. The tanning and video watching had been happening at his house the past few days, and it was getting exhausting to keep up her perfect girlfriend persona. Biting back her replies to his idiotic comments, pretending not to understand his suggestive comments about taking their relationship 'to the next level' and 'making the most of the summer.' Yuck. Just a few more days, she told herself, and she'd start slipping in mentions of her chats with Logan to see how Spencer reacted.

Beyond the helpful Spencer escape, going to a worksite meant that her dad was finally back at work after a weirdly long break. Plus, she loved seeing all the houses he built. She had no interest in building or construction, but the architecture and decorating were always gorgeous.

And—though she'd never admit this to any of her friends—she really liked spending time with her dad. She'd had her parents all to herself since Di had gone away to California but it wasn't the same during the school year. There was cheerleading, her dad worked all the time, and her mom was always busy with charity events. Summers were slower, and this one even more than usual with so many of her friends getting summer jobs. The unexpected visit to a worksite excited her probably a little too much, but the combination of time with her dad and break from Spencer was irresistible.

As Cassie walked around the nearly finished house, the carpets covered in builder's plastic and the walls unpainted, she couldn't help thinking about Spencer, however. The house was way more his style than hers. She liked the rustic, antique look of her family's lake house. She always felt a little uncomfortable at his with its modern lines and sleek decoration. Or maybe it was just his family she felt uncomfortable around. They were so clearly fake and so clearly obsessed with the same stupid superficial stuff as her parents and everyone else they knew. Cassie fit right in with them, that's what made her the most uncomfortable.

Looking around the new house, she noticed a few things out of place, and bit her lip. Should she say something?

Her father was talking to one of the guys on site, nodding and looking at some notes with a frown on his face.

"Dad?" Cassie called him over. He looked up, his grumpy expression gone when he caught her eye. "Is this supposed to be like this?"

She was pointing to an opening in a wall that could have been a window except it was facing an interior wall. Her dad's face clouded over and he turned back to the man. He started shouting and waving his hands.

Cassie felt a slight twinge of pity for the guy getting chewed out. She hadn't meant to get him in trouble, but she was used to being on sites with her dad, and he'd taught her how things should look towards the end.

"Sorry about that," he said, coming over to give her shoulders a squeeze. "I thought Jimmy could handle this one on his own so I could have a break, but it looks like he couldn't."

"Are you going back to work?" Cassie asked as they made their way to the car. The secret reason she was excited to tag along with him was because he always took her to get ice cream after a site visit, ever since she was little. She knew now these visits had started as a way to keep her occupied during school breaks, and the ice cream was her reward for behaving herself. But it was so much a part of their ritual, she didn't want to break it to him an eighteen-year-old cheerleader wasn't quite as excited about ice cream as an eight-year-old in pigtails.

"No, I have a bit more vacation time to use." He wasn't quite looking her in the eyes when he said it.

"Why are you taking so much time off this year?" Cassie didn't mean for it to sound accusatory, but it had been bugging her the more she thought about it. He'd never taken more than a few days here and there, maybe a week max for the Fourth of July. It had been almost a month now.

Her dad looked at her, right in the eyes this time.

"It's my last summer with my little girl at home," he said, a sad smile on his face. Cassie's heart melted a little. "I saved up a lot of days over the years. Might as well use them all now before summer internships in the Big Apple lure you away."

Others may have had the urge to roll her eyes at his corniness, but Cassie beamed at him as they got in the car.

"So," her dad said as he started the engine. "Were you able to help the Hanes boy?"

She looked at him, but his eyes were on the road. He didn't turn to look at her.

How much did he really want to know?

"I think so," she said, tugging on the end of her ponytail. "I drove him to the doctor."

"Anything serious?"

She shook her head.

"Dislocated shoulder."

Her dad grunted a little.

"He's going to Columbia."

He raised his eyebrows, eyes still on the road.

"I said since you and Mom are alumni, we could answer some questions for him."

"You can answer them Cass." His voice was low and hard. "I have nothing to do with this. This is your mess to clean up."

The bright feeling from just a few minutes earlier disappeared in a puff of dark smoke. Even though she'd always intended to be the one to talk to Logan about Columbia, there had been a tiny hope that her dad would maybe be able to answer some questions, too.

"That's what I meant, I would answer them," she said quietly, and turned to look out the window, her stomach in knots. "Like you said, make sure he's happy, right?"

Her dad said nothing. An icy silence washed over the car that hung over them until they got to the ice cream parlor. As much as she'd been looking forward to it, the ice cream wasn't quite the treat she'd been expecting.

BACK AT HOME, Cassie's dad disappeared into his office,

telling her not to disturb him for the rest of the afternoon. Cassie set herself up in the living room with a face mask and *Real Housewives*. But she couldn't concentrate on the show.

Her thoughts drifted to Logan, and she worried that things wouldn't work out the way her dad wanted. Logan hadn't replied to her last message from two days ago. Had it been too flirty? Had the winking emoji been too much? She never normally hesitated about stuff like that, but she didn't really know him. Was he the kind of guy who liked a girl joking around? He probably preferred a more serious girl.

Not that she cared what kind of girl he liked.

But she needed to know a little bit about him for this whole thing to work. She went through what she did know. He was a waiter at Chez Pierre. He rode a bike—an old one but well maintained. He was staying with his aunt and uncle this summer.

None of this was going to help her plans for the summer. What else?

She knew he liked to do things for himself. He'd made that as clear as possible. It seemed like in this case she'd have to let him take the lead and he'd tell her how she could help him.

But she always let others take the lead and tell her what to do. For once in her life, she wanted to be the one to decide how things went.

Her phone buzzed and she looked down to see yet another text from Spencer. She rolled her eyes and didn't bother answering. Spencer was more than happy to tell Cassie what he wanted, as often as possible and in increasingly annoying ways. Cassie used the excuse of dinner with her dad to avoid seeing him last night, but she knew she couldn't avoid Spencer forever. That was part of why she was so eager to see Logan again so the 'get Spencer to break up with her' plan could finally get started.

After all, this was all about the plan, and had nothing to do with Logan's damn dimple that she couldn't stop thinking about. The small smile he'd given her had lit up his face, and made Brittney's online swooning a little more understandable.

Her phone buzzed again and she let out a curse as she peeled off her face mask. It was impossible to relax at home. Instead of spending any more energy thinking about how irritating Spencer was or how distracting Logan's dimple was, Cassie decided to fall back into her default time-wasting pick-me-up activity, treasured by entitled teens since the beginning of time.

She would go shopping.

Starting with one of the local art galleries was a strategic decision. There was no way Spencer would be there or even in the neighborhood. He wasn't into art at all; he didn't even pretend to enjoy it like his dad did. The Huntington houses were covered in all sorts of rare finds that Cassie always wanted to ask about, but she didn't want to look like an idiot in front of his parents. She didn't know much, just what she liked and didn't like.

No one knew, not even Marissa, but Cassie was hoping to major in art history. Her parents wanted her to major in business, or law, or something 'useful.' But she had seen firsthand that a degree like that didn't really matter. At all of the charity events she attended with her mom, no one seemed to have taken a straight path to their success. Some hadn't even gone to college! Sometimes she felt like the only reason she was going to college at all was because it would make her parents proud.

So she might as well study something she liked while she was there, right? Her mind flitted briefly to Logan, wondering what he would major in, but she stopped herself. She was at the gallery to distract her from all of that.

"Cassie!"

A huge smile spread across her face when she saw who had

called out. Distraction had arrived in an even better form than browsing one of her favorite spaces. Marissa was walking into the gallery.

"Marissa! You made it back!"

Her best friend let out a squeal as she maneuvered around sculpture display cases to hug her. The gallery owner gave them the evil eye, so Cassie hurried her back outside. The warm sun lifted Cassie's mood even more. The two girls linked arms and headed to the coffee shop down the street. It was just like so many other summer days they'd had over the years. Heaviness spread through Cassie's chest when she realized there were actually very few of these days left for the two of them.

"Why didn't you tell me you were coming?"

"I wanted to surprise you. I blew off work for the rest of the week."

"Can you do that?" Cassie had never had a part-time job—had never needed one.

Marissa shrugged.

"I told them I was sick. And I am! I feel wretched for leaving you alone the other day. Were you super bored?"

Cassie didn't let her smile slip as her stomach gave a lurch.

"No, it was fine."

"What did you end up doing? Have you been hanging out with Spencer?"

Cassie nodded but didn't elaborate. They'd arrived at the coffee shop and there was no line, so they ordered right away.

As they were waiting for their drinks, Marissa launched into the story of why her mom had made such a big deal about coming home right away for some relative's birthday party. Cassie's phone buzzed, and she rolled her eyes as she pulled it out, expecting another text from Spencer begging her to come over. At least now she could invite Marissa along and she wouldn't have to be alone with him.

But it was Logan.

Hey can I ask you a question about the food in New York?

A smile tugged at the corners of her lips. She had still been worried about coming on too strong the other day. He probably just wasn't used to girls flirting with him—not that she had been, of course. Just being friendly.

That depends. Did you get your prescription filled?

An eye rolling emoji was her only response.

"Is that Spencer? Do you need to go?" Marissa pouted a little and Cassie realized her smile had gotten bigger. She quickly pursed her lips and slipped her phone back into her bag.

"No, not Spencer."

Marissa's eyes grew wide.

"Is it someone else?"

Cassie couldn't help but smile again, a brilliant idea flashing through her mind. She'd been trying to figure out a way for Spencer to find out that she was hanging out with Logan, and here was Marissa, the one person who wouldn't hesitate to jump on an opening in their relationship.

"It's just Logan Hanes," she said, her tone coming out the perfect mix of excited but trying to sound casual. She was impressed with herself at how easily she was able to pretend.

Marissa wrinkled her nose.

"Why are you hanging out with him?" she asked as she grabbed her glass full of iced coffee.

Cassie frowned and took her iced tea. In order for her interest to seem genuine, Logan had to sound interesting. But so far she didn't even know anything interesting about him, besides that distracting dimple.

"He's going to Columbia. It's an incoming freshman thing."

"Oh." Marissa frowned. "So you decided, then? Definitely Columbia?"

Cassie's heart sank, realizing what she'd just done. This wasn't how she'd planned on telling Marissa. And had Cassie officially decided? Her dad hadn't even pushed earlier in the car when she'd mentioned Columbia, the way he usually did whenever the topic was mentioned. But to Marissa, what else could this mean?

"I...don't know yet. But just in case, this is part of the requirements." That sounded lame even to her ears, but Marissa didn't seem to notice. She was looking at Cassie with wide eyes and downturned lips.

"I just really hoped to be at Missoula with you in the fall." Marissa stuck out her lower lip and shifted in her seat. Cassie busied herself with her tea, slowly stirring two packets of sugar into it. It was never sweet enough for her. "I thought we had it all worked out? We'd share an off campus apartment and pledge a sorority in the spring. It'll be like high school but better."

Cassie finally looked up.

"Better than high school? Is that even possible?" She raised an eyebrow and Marissa let out a giggle. "It was pretty crazy fun, right?"

Marissa nodded.

Cassie took a deep breath.

"I guess I just want something different maybe than four more years of that."

There, she'd said it. Marissa was her best friend. If she couldn't say it to her, who could she say it to?

But Marissa was staring open-mouthed at her with her brow wrinkled.

"I don't understand. You don't want four more years of having fun? Of being popular? Of dating the hottest guy in school?"

Cassie opened her mouth, not even sure what she could say to that, when her phone buzzed again and saved her. Glancing away from Marissa's flabbergasted face, she swiped it open eagerly, thinking it may be Logan again. But it was Spencer this time, wondering what her plans were for the day. The desire to shake things up flitted away, as if it had never really been there to begin with.

"Speaking of hot guys, should we finish up and go hang out with Spencer? Make high school last a little longer?" Cassie held back a laugh at how bright and bubbly Marissa got at the mention of Spencer's name.

As they left the coffee shop, Cassie let out a sigh, however, as she mentally prepared for yet another afternoon and evening like so many others before. Everyone else seemed to want life to go on the way it was. Why couldn't she be satisfied with the same thing? She knew it was a good life. She wished she could just be happy about it like everyone else.

____

CHAPTER TEN

IT WAS Logan's second night back at the restaurant and things weren't going very well. He'd been slow the previous night, but luckily so had the restaurant. He'd been able to get by on half speed, taking his time delivering orders and getting the others to help him out a bit. It had cost him a share of his tips, but it was worth it to keep his job.

Tonight, however, it looked like he might lose his job after all if he didn't pick up the pace. There was no way that he'd be able to perform as well as he usually did. His shoulder still hurt and he didn't want to take too much of the medication the doctor had given him. He'd already taken a lot during the day to get through his cleaning routines. This was his third summer working for the same company, so they knew him and were willing to go easy on him for a few days, but this was also peak season. If he couldn't keep up, that would be a second job he couldn't afford to lose.

Maybe he should have taken up Hideki on his offer to work at the boat house, he thought as he looked at the growing line of people in front of the greeter's stand waiting to be seated. But he couldn't just sit around all day behind a counter, checking boats in and out. He had to move. It felt wrong to just sit around. It was yet one more reason he knew New York would be right for him. The city that never sleeps. The energy was palpable even in photographs and lit a fire in him just thinking about it.

Besides, the more experience he got as a waiter, the better, since that's probably what he'd end up doing while he was there. It was all totally manageable: classes during the day, then working nights and weekends. He was getting so excited about leaving he could hardly sleep at night.

Which was also not helping his performance at work. His manager, Tony, caught him staring off into space and made a jerking motion with his head. Logan's stomach sank and with a quick glance at his tables—how had he gotten two more already?—he slinked into the kitchen behind Tony.

The kitchen was noisy, hot and busy, filled to the brim with people and smells. It was overpowering and stimulated all five senses at once.

Logan loved it.

He did not love how Tony was glaring at him.

"What is going on tonight?" Tony crossed his arms over his chest. "Is your arm still bothering you?"

"A bit," Logan admitted, trying not to reach up to touch it. He was supposed to be wearing his sling but there was no way he could do that here. He just kept it close to his body and tried not to bump into anyone or anything.

"Well how long is it going to be that way? We're getting into the busy season. I need all hands on deck."

"I know, it'll be fine in a few days, I promise." Logan knew it would be more like a few weeks, but he'd always been a fast healer. His mom wouldn't have even known about half the things he'd done with Hideki if his aunt hadn't filled her in. The bruises and scars had always faded by the time he'd returned home at the end of summer.

"Well, it better be," Tony said with a cold stare, and then waved him away.

Tail between his legs, Logan turned to head back out, grabbing a plate from the counter as he went, trying to be as useful as possible.

So, of course, he ran straight into someone else in his rush to leave the kitchen.

The clatter of plates and yells drew the stares of all the patrons in the vicinity. Looking around, Logan saw that three of the curious stares were Cassie, Spencer, and a curly haired girl Logan thought was named either Melissa or Marissa.

And they were sitting in his section.

Perfect. Like this night could get any worse.

After apologizing profusely to his coworker, who was covered in sauce and glaring at him, Logan hurried over to Cassie's table.

She was looking very hard at her menu. Her long hair was swept up in a complicated knot on her head with a few strands falling out to frame her face. Logan took a deep breath and tried to ignore the temptation to brush one behind her ear. He barely knew her. She hadn't even replied to his request for information on New York; she'd just bugged him again about his shoulder stuff. She obviously saw him as some charity case, which was fine with him. He didn't need this alumni match thing anyway. He spent enough time with annoying rich people at this job; he didn't need to spend any more time with her.

Then she looked up he found himself lost in the intense green forest of her eyes.

"Hi," he drawled slowly, his face splitting into a grin. He'd completely forgotten whatever he was about to say. Cassie looked down quickly, her face cool and blank.

Logan cleared his throat, looking at Marissa instead. "Welcome to Chez Pierre. I'm Logan, I'll be taking care of you tonight." Marissa's eyes widened slightly, and a small smile appeared on her face. "Can I start you all off with some drinks?"

"Yeah, I'll have a margarita, please," said Spencer. Logan let out a short laugh, but Spencer's face was stony.

"You're not serious? Spencer, we've been in the same school for four years. I know you're not twenty-one."

Spencer's face clouded over, and he stared at Logan, who stared right back. Yes the Huntingtons were important, and if Spencer had been with his dad, Logan might not have said anything. He let plenty of things slide at the restaurant for the VIP customers, as per Tony's orders. But this was just ballsy and stupid and Logan was on the verge of losing his job as it was. Serving underage customers would mean he wouldn't be working in restaurants for a long time.

"Spencer, stop being an asshole," Cassie said, not looking up from her menu. She'd been studying it closely, as if to commit the entire thing to memory. "Just a round of Diet Cokes, please."

Her tone was dismissive but in the last second before he turned to go, she looked up at him, and rolled her eyes in Spencer's direction. Relief washed over Logan.

"I'll be right back with that for you."

"And some bread!" Spencer called as he walked away.

The rest of the evening was uneventful with no more secret looks from Cassie. He might have even imagined it. Maybe she'd been rolling her eyes at Marissa. Maybe she'd been rolling her eyes about him, not Spencer. As the evening wore on, he became more and more frustrated with himself. All he needed from her was information on New York, nothing else. Why should he care that her boyfriend was a jerk? Or what color her eyes were? Or how she shivered slightly in her tank top every few minutes with no sign from Spencer that he was about to give her his jacket?

Finally, Logan was delivering the last tray of plates to his last table. Cassie's table had been taking forever to finish up. He'd also been going by less often than he usually did, but he already knew not to expect much, if any, tip from Spencer. It wasn't worth his time to check in on them.

As he was walking back to the kitchen with the empty tray, he glanced over his shoulder at their table, and ran straight into someone coming out from the kitchen. For the second time that night, the explosion of plates crashing drew the stares of tables around them. Unfortunately, this time it also drew Tony over.

"Logan, I'm sorry, that's it." He said, his voice just loud enough for people to hear. "This isn't working out. I'm sorry. You can come by for your last paycheck tomorrow morning."

Cold shock ripped through him like he'd just jumped into the lake in January. Hot on its heels was a burning shame that he hoped would burn through the floor so he could fall down the hole it would make.

Even from where he was sitting on the floor, Logan could hear Spencer laughing. Marissa let out a chuckle. Logan didn't look to see if Cassie smiled. It didn't matter, he told himself as he stood up and brushed himself off. She didn't have to accept him. None of them did. Columbia already had.

But when took a final look at her table, there was a small smile on her lips that ripped his heart into shreds.

CHAPTER ELEVEN

CASSIE WASN'T sure why she'd done it. Maybe it had been the look on Logan's face. Completely crushed did not even begin to describe it. Had she ever felt that way about anything? Had she ever wanted something so badly—needed it so badly—that having it taken away would do that to her?

The simple answer was no. And that's what she so desperately wanted to change.

It was the look on Spencer's face that pushed her over the edge, however. The pure pleasure at someone else's pain made her stomach churn. Marissa was clearly torn, her eyebrows turned down in concern while a half smile played on her lips. When Spencer saw Cassie's unamused pursed lips and arched brow, he turned his laughing face to Marissa, looking for someone to share in his glee. Marissa giggled and Cassie swallowed the urge to throw something at them both.

Cassie knew she should be happy about this pushing the two of them together, but all she could think about was Logan. He had been struggling all night. He hid it well, but there was no doubt he was slower, though he made up for it at his other tables with his chatter and smiles. He had avoided Cassie's table like the plague once he'd dropped off their plates—slightly cold due to how long it took him to bring them out. Spencer had complained, of course.

She tried to tell herself that it wasn't her fault Logan got fired. He could have taken a sick day. He had medication to help with the pain. But shame spread through her as she watched him pick himself up off the floor and head into the back, his head drooping. Why was seeing him in so much pain doing such a number on her? She'd seen countless athletes take worse hits on the field. Spencer had even cried once and she'd just felt annoyed.

But Logan hadn't signed up for bodily harm. That part really was her fault. And she couldn't fix it with a ride to the doctor's or a few hundred for a bill. She'd been counting on leaving him a large tip and now she couldn't even do that.

"Cass!" Spencer was calling to her, waving his arms in front of her face. "Let's go. He forgot to bring us the check so let's bail."

"Absolutely not." Cassie crossed her arms over her chest and stared him down. "Why are you such an asshole, Spencer?"

"And why are you such a spoiled princess? I didn't even want to come to this fancy place, you did."

"Why does it matter? You can afford it."

Marissa looked from one to the other through lowered lids, her phone held tightly in her two hands as if she were texting and not completely absorbed in their fight. Cassie's irritation at her best friend was almost tied with her frustration with Spencer.

"Whatever, can we just go?" Spencer pushed back his chair and stood up.

"I need to do something first." Cassie stood up before she

could think twice about what she was going to do. She made her way over to the greeter's station.

"Excuse me, is the manager here?" she asked quietly, thinking of how her mother always handled things like this. Quiet, calm, polite. Never angry or demanding. Hopefully at least something in her life besides her money could help Logan out. The greeter ran off and came back with the same mustachioed man who had fired Logan so cruelly in front of everyone. He introduced himself with a level of simpering that was a bit exaggerated considering she was still a teenager.

"I'm sorry for all the noise tonight, miss. Was everything to your liking?"

"Actually, no," she said, and looked straight up at him. Now it was time to use something from her father's handbook. Look them right in the eyes, let them know who's boss. "I don't appreciate the way you fired that young man just now."

"He was not performing to the Chez Pierre standards we know our valued customers expect."

"It looked like he was injured?"

"Yes, and not performing to the level needed."

"Was an alternative job offered to him?"

"An alternative...?" The manager frowned.

Cassie had heard her dad talk about this recently and it gave her the inklings of an idea.

"When an employee has a disability, even temporarily, the employer should make a reasonable accommodation for him. That could mean a different job."

The manager stared at her with his lips pressed tightly together. He cleared his throat.

"That's not what the law actually—"

"All I saw here," Cassie interrupted him, raising her voice just a bit so the tables nearest the doors could hear. "Was an employer disregarding the needs of an employee with a disability."

The manager's eyebrows popped up, his face going white. Cassie wasn't sure that was technically the way the law worked, but she'd heard her dad complain enough to know the laws were there to keep people from getting fired just for being injured.

"I assure you if there was something he was able to do here, I would have offered." His tone was slightly less slick now, eager to end the conversation.

"What about bartender? Did you offer him that?" Cassie was pleased with her spontaneous suggestion. He'd make way more tips as a bartender than a server.

"I will make whatever personnel decisions are best for the establishment, don't you worry." His eyes narrowed. "Young lady."

"Well, thank you," Cassie said, turning on the sweet charm again, despite her urge to smack the man. She waved over Spencer and Marissa. "I'm sure Mr. Huntington will be pleased to hear it as well."

For the second time, the manager paled. If he didn't recognize Spencer, he certainly recognized his name.

"Was everything to your liking tonight, Mr. Huntington?" It was like the guy had a 'sucking up' light switch inside of him.

Spencer shrugged.

"It was okay."

Spencer's grip was tight on her arm. They all smiled and thanked the manager, as he wished them a good evening. Spencer didn't let go of her until they were in front of his car.

"That's what was so important? Sticking up for that nerd?" Spencer spat as they got into his car.

Cassie sighed.

"Just take me home, I'm tired."

"But I want to go out." His voice was half whine, half

command. It was how he said most things, she suddenly realized.

"I could stay out a bit longer," Marissa piped up from the back seat.

"Great! You can take me home, then," Cassie said and closed her eyes. "You'll still have company on your next bender."

"Geez, Cass, what is up with you lately?" Spencer said. "You're no fun anymore."

She opened her eyes to take in his over-gelled hair and 300 dollar t-shirt.

"I just think it's time to grow up, that's all. We're eighteen. We're going to college in a few months. We're adults now."

"Ugh, you sound like my dad."

"Gee, thanks. Nice of you to call your girlfriend a stuck-up old douchebag."

"So that's what you think of my dad?" Spencer's voice was suddenly high-pitched.

"Spencer, calm down. You say the same thing about your dad all the time."

"You should show a little respect after all he's done for you."

"What's that supposed to mean?" Now Cassie's voice was high-pitched. She barely registered Marissa in the back seat, who had shrunk down as small as possible next to the window. She was staring out into the street, as if she couldn't hear the fight they were having. It wasn't the first one Marissa had seen, not even the first of the evening, but this somehow felt like the worst one they'd had. Ever.

"If you only knew..." Spencer trailed off and shook his head. "He's done everything for you."

"What? How could he possibly have anything to do with my life?" The anger radiated off of Cassie's chest as the words flowed out. "I'm the one that got into Columbia, with my grades.

My brain. Not some sports scholarship to a school my daddy had to donate a million dollars to so they'd let me in."

It wasn't true, and Cassie knew it. But she was suddenly over being nice. Being what everyone expected of her. A month ago she would have gone out with them, found a bar, a party, anything. There was still time to break up with him later, she'd told herself. But tonight suddenly seemed like the perfect night to do it.

Instead of yelling back, Spencer laughed—a harsh, rough sound that grated on Cassie's last nerve.

"My dad's not the only one going to have to fork over millions."

"What the hell are you talking about? Either tell me or admit you know nothing and get over yourself."

"No, I don't think I'll tell you anything." Spencer smirked as he pulled up in front of Cassie's house. "It's best you hear it from your dad. Let him explain why you all should be groveling at my dad's feet."

"Whatever," said Cassie, opening the car door. "Don't bother telling me anything anymore. It's over." She got out and leaned back in, staring him down, daring him to ask her to change her mind. "Come on, Marissa."

Her best friend hadn't moved an inch from her crouched position by the window in the backseat. She looked at Cassie with downcast eyes, biting her lip. Cassie took a deep breath and told herself it didn't matter who Marissa chose. This was what she'd wanted, after all, to get rid of Spencer and get the two of them together instead.

But tonight she really needed her best friend.

When Marissa didn't move from the backseat after a long and tense minute of silence, Cassie slammed the door shut and ran up the path to the front door without looking back.

She burst into the house, scanning for signs of her father.

She'd deal with Marissa later. Right now, she had to find out what Spencer meant.

"Dad!" her panicked voice rang through the house, bouncing off the walls in unlit rooms.

"What is it?" he came running out of his office, still dressed. Cassie stopped short. It was nearly ten at night; he was usually getting ready for bed at this hour.

"Are you going out tonight?" she asked, narrowing her eyes and looking closer at his clothes. They were nicer than the old baseball jerseys and cargo shorts he'd been wearing most of the summer so far.

"I had a dinner meeting with a client," he said.

"Oh." That made sense. What else could it have been?

"Is everything okay? You sound upset." His brow was furrowed.

She shook her head, remembering everything Spencer had said.

"I got into a fight with Spencer." She sniffed, and tears started pooling in the corners of her eyes. She blinked them back.

"What did you do?" The shift from concern to accusation was instant.

"I didn't do anything!" Cassie cried, crossing her arms over her chest. "He was being a jerk about me not wanting to go out after dinner. I told him I didn't want this summer to be like high school."

He dad nodded and smiled. She basked a bit in the pride of finally doing something right.

"But then he said something about the Huntingtons." She tried to keep her voice even, but the tears threatened to spill over at any moment. "And how we owe them something?"

Her dad just shook his head, frowning. She held her breath.

Spencer had talked about her dad owing someone millions, but it couldn't be that bad, could it?

"It's just a few introductions his dad made for me. It's not a big deal."

Her heart lifted, and she took a deep shuddering breath to calm herself.

"Really?"

"Yes, it was all for business." Her dad shook his head. "Spencer was obviously angry about something else and wanted to upset you."

"Well, it worked." Cassie let out her deep breath in a loud whoosh.

"I'm sure you'll work it out. He's a great kid."

Cassie bit her lip. She was pretty sure they'd broken up. The words lay on the tip of her tongue, wanting to be let out. But the look on her dad's face stopped her.

For the first time she could remember, he looked old. Not gray hair and a walker old. Just tired, with new wrinkles around his eyes, and bags under them like he hadn't been sleeping enough.

But he also looked proud, as he usually did when there was talk of Spencer. And she lived for those looks. She tried so hard and seemed to be failing so far this summer, at least where Logan was concerned. Letting her dad know about Spencer would be failing all over again.

"I'm sure we will." She gave her dad a hug. "Good night."

She walked into her bedroom and shut the door.

Before she could think too hard about it, she sent a quick message to Logan.

Sorry about tonight.

She wanted to say more, about what a jerk Spencer was, and how she'd once been humiliated in front of the entire cheerleading team freshman year when she'd worn the wrong color socks. But that didn't seem like a similar situation, when she thought about it. Besides, she didn't really know him that well. She wasn't supposed to be sharing stuff like that. Just about Columbia. Her dad wanted her to seem nice, not overbearing and crazy.

It's fine. I'll live. His reply came a few minutes later.

Still, it's not cool your boss fired you like that in front of everyone. Cassie wanted to say more, but couldn't find the words to tell him just how terrible she felt.

She didn't think Logan would reply, but another message came a few minutes later.

Actually, he just called to offer me a bartending job. I start tomorrow at 6.

Cassie swelled with a strange mix of pride and pleasure that she'd never experienced before. It was different than what she'd just felt with her dad. Most of the time when she was this pleased with herself, it was for something she'd done that everyone knew about. This was the first time no one knew.

And they couldn't know. If Logan found out about her interfering with his job, he may start to question why she was helping him in the first place.

Her pride was quickly smothered by anxiety. So she did what she usually did when her nerves started up and made a joke.

Awesome. So I guess I can call on you for all my keg parties now?

A rolling eye emoji was the only reply. She grinned and put down her phone to get ready for bed. She didn't think once about Spencer while brushing her teeth, or worry about Marissa in between putting on her pajamas and snuggling under her comforter.

Instead, she fell asleep with a smile on her face and Logan

on her brain, telling herself that, with a few tweaks, her master plan for this summer could get back on track.

LESS THAN 24 hours later Cassie was in front of Logan's house, her hand poised over the door, ready to knock. She still wasn't entirely sure what she was doing there, but it meant avoiding thinking about Spencer.

Given that she hadn't heard from him since he'd dropped her off, apparently they really had broken up. She hadn't heard from Marissa either, which was harder to accept. In her original plan, after all, Cassie had wanted Spencer to break up with her in order to get together with Marissa. Then Cassie could graciously encourage her friend to go out with her ex. Dumping him in front of Marissa made Cassie look like the jerk. She decided to hope that something was finally happening between the two of them, rather than get too angry with her best friend for abandoning her.

Still, Cassie had spent most of the day eating ice cream and watching bad TV. Around four that afternoon she'd gotten it into her head that she should offer Logan a ride to work, so she could ask more about what the manager had said. What if he'd mentioned why he'd given Logan the bartending job? Cassie had to be sure that her secret was safe. At least, that's what she told herself as she stood paralyzed in front of Logan's door.

After taking a deep breath of courage, she lifted her hand again to knock when it opened. She stepped back, surprised, and stumbled a little. A strong arm shot out to pull her back upright.

"Woah," said Logan, still gripping her arm. Her body was now only inches away from his. She could smell his shampoo and see the little flecks of gold in his brown eyes. "What are you doing here?"

Cassie took a step back and blinked up at him, her mouth opening once without words coming out. He didn't let go of her arm, and she realized she didn't want him to. He didn't look mad, just surprised, which gave her the final boost she needed to speak.

"I came to give you a ride to work." She flashed him a grin that hopefully hid the slight tremor in her voice.

"Thank the hot cheerleading gods, I can go back to my game now!" a voice called out from inside the house.

His cousin stuck his head out the door and smiled.

"She seems pretty cool, Logan, not sure why you were complaining so much about her."

Logan turned bright red. He dropped her arm and shoved his cousin back through the door.

Cassie felt her own face flush, but she wasn't sure why. She was just helping Logan out. Like she'd promised her dad.

"Ready to go?" She held up her keys and jingled them.

He just nodded and followed her to her car.

"So what kind of complaints did you have?" she teased as they were buckling themselves in.

"It's nothing." He was turning a bright red. "I'm sorry. I shouldn't be saying anything. You've been nothing but nice to me."

Her smile faltered.

"That's not entirely true."

"Oh?"

Her heart was pounding at his quirked eyebrow and slightly tilted head.

"I should have stuck up for you in front of Spencer. I acted like I didn't even know you. That was rude."

He shrugged, but she saw a small smile and the merest hint of the dimple appear on his face.

"It's no big deal," Logan said. "We don't really know each other, you know?"

"Well the whole point of this match thing is to change that." Cassie's chipper cheerleader voice filled the car.

"I thought the match was supposed to be with your father?"

Crap! Cassie could barely keep the lies straight, apparently. With Marissa, her father, and now Logan. But it felt worse to lie to Logan.

This was a chance to finally have someone see her for herself and not the spoiled cheerleader or Spencer's girlfriend or the daughter of Mr. and Mrs. Hart. She wanted him to know her as she really was, not her fake persona. It scared her, but with everything that had happened last night, it was at least something that felt like going in the right direction.

"Yeah but what good does it do to get to know an alum?" She winked at him, then immediately felt like an idiot. "You're not going to school with him, are you?"

Logan nodded slowly.

"So what do you want to know?" he asked. "There isn't much to tell. I'd rather hear more about New York."

Cassie sighed. They were nearly at the restaurant. It was probably pointless to try to change how he saw her at this point. First impressions were hard to get over.

"We can pick this up on the way home, okay?" she said as they pulled into the parking lot.

Logan shook his head and unbuckled his seatbelt.

"No, really, you've done plenty. I can't keep bumming rides off of you all summer."

"Well, it does interfere with my partying schedule," she said with a wink. He laughed, and a happy pool of light spread through her stomach. It felt good to be around him. It was nothing like the bored attention she gave to Spencer, or even the giddy gossiping with Marissa. Both of which were apparently over now. If this was the alternative for the summer, it wouldn't be that bad.

"I'll see you later then?" He looked at her with hopeful eyes, and she couldn't help but grin.

"I can't wait."

CHAPTER TWELVE

WHEN LOGAN'S mother showed up halfway through his shift to surprise him, he was happy. Really. But he was a tiny bit bummed that it meant no ride from Cassie. Not that he'd been looking forward to it or anything.

Looks like I won't need that ride, my mom showed up. He texted her as soon as his mom walked through the door.

Have fun! Cassie sent several smiley faces along with her message.

And you can too tonight now that you don't need to drive me around. Logan knew someone like her must have better things to do than be his chauffeur.

Yes, super fun watching baseball with my dad.

He smiled at her sleeping emoji.

"Who's got you smiling like that?" his mom was sitting at the bar, sipping the Shirley Temple he'd made her. His mom never drank, so he hadn't grown up knowing anything about drinking besides the random beers he and Hideki would sneak sometimes whenever he was up at the lake. The one thing he was actually dying to ask Cassie was about keg parties. He was slightly worried about going to his first one and not knowing any of the unspoken rules. That probably wasn't the kind of information Columbia intended to be shared through this match program, so maybe it was a good thing her dad was too busy to be the one to meet with him this summer.

"No one," Logan said, shoving the phone in his pocket.

"It's not the Hart girl, is it?" His mom kept her voice even, but he knew her tones well enough to tell she was not very happy about it.

"It's Columbia stuff. You wouldn't understand."

Her face fell and Logan felt like an ass.

"That came out wrong, I'm sorry."

"No, it's fine." She shook her head, staring down into her pink drink. "You're right. There will be a lot of things I can't teach you about that world. I just wish there was someone else who you could talk to about it besides her."

The question was burning on his tongue, dying to be asked. Why not Cassie? But he decided to just drop it. Just like knowing what all his mom's voice tones secretly meant, Logan knew the best ways to keep her happy. Changing topics away from upsetting things worked every time.

"How are my bartending skills so far?" He gestured at the mostly empty bar. It had been a slow night, so perfect for learning the ropes from the regular bartender. He didn't seem that upset about having to split his shifts with Logan. Apparently he had been begging Tony for weeks to train someone else so he could get a few days off.

"Well, this is good. What else can you make?"

Logan started rattling off everything he'd learned, and his mom seemed to relax a little. He hoped she wasn't working too hard this summer. He was really looking forward to the extra money he'd be able to pull in as a bartender. Maybe he'd even be able to surprise her with a ticket to New York to help him move in.

As much as he hated to admit it, maybe getting run off the road hadn't been the worst thing to happen this summer. He was still furious at whoever had done it, but he was starting to let go of that a little bit. It had been painful in the moment, but there was finally a silver lining.

IT HAD BEEN three days since his mom's surprise visit and Logan had almost convinced himself that Cassie was just another friend. Someone he could call for a ride—which he hadn't, not yet—or someone he could talk to about regular stuff.

He still hadn't dared ask her more than just things about New York, but it had gotten a little more personal in his messages now, though not entirely on purpose.

What's your favorite park in New York? he asked one day during a break cleaning houses.

Bryant Park, she'd replied seconds later.

No need to think about it? He'd been surprised by her quick response.

Nope. My first kiss was there.

He stared at the phone, questions swirling in his mind. Was she saying that just to be honest? Or to make him think about kissing? He shook his head. Why would she want him to do that? He wanted to ask if it had been Spencer, but Logan knew that was dumb for so many reasons.

First, they weren't that kind of friends—at least, he didn't think so. He didn't actually have many friends that were girls. He'd been so focused on school the past four years, and summers were spent up at the lake doing jobs not many girls his age did.

Second, she'd only been with Spencer since the beginning of senior year, and she'd obviously dated boys before that. His lack of experience with friends as girls was nothing compared to his total lack of experience with an actual girlfriend. It's not even something he'd really thought about. Even if he had dared to ask someone out, he didn't exactly have the extra cash, let alone a car, to take a girl anywhere.

In the end, he decided not to reply to her first kiss revelation, and told himself he wouldn't think about it anymore. It was pointless to think about kissing someone he barely knew. Someone with a boyfriend. Someone totally not interested in him like that.

Someone whose green eyes crinkled up adorably at the edges when she smiled.

His phone buzzed, and he shook his head to clear his thoughts of her eyes and lips and other pointless things.

What do you think you'll major in?

He frowned. So she was just going to ignore the fact that the word "kiss" was sitting there, in the message above? That's fine, he could, too. Because he was definitely not thinking about it anymore.

They have a good math program. What about you?

Partying, obviously.

He rolled his eyes and got back to work. It was the perfect opening to ask his questions about what to expect at a college party, but she clearly wasn't in a very serious mood at the moment. He had yet to see her serious about anything other than bugging him about his shoulder. With a sigh, he realized she didn't *have* to be serious about anything. She'd probably be off at parties while he spent every weekend doing what he was doing now. Working.

It would all be worth it though, he reminded himself as he bent to start scrubbing his tenth toilet of the day.

———

CONSIDERING the effort he spent over the next twenty four hours to not think about her, Cassie was the last person Logan expected to walk in the door of the house he was cleaning. When he saw her dad was with her, however, things clicked into place. This was a brand new house, just completed, with a giant 'Hart & Preston builders' sign out front. The cleaning company Logan worked for has been hired to take care of all the dust and dirt the workers had left behind. Of course the developer would want to come see how they were doing.

Logan realized he'd actually seen Mr. Hart before, at other houses in previous summers. But he definitely would have remembered seeing Cassie with him.

Logan kept his head down, however, as a flash of blond hair whipped past him. Her father walked around, inspecting the finishes and pointing things out to Cassie. She sounded interested and even made a few comments that her dad seemed to appreciate.

As an odd tingling spread through his chest, Logan told himself he should go introduce himself. This was a perfect opportunity to network with an alumnus, and one who already knew who he was. But he looked down at his grubby clothes and dirty hands and hurried off to somewhere less visible.

"Hey." Not five minutes later, Logan heard Cassie's voice behind him and turned, a bottle of furniture polish in one hand and a filthy rag in the other.

"What are you doing here?" he asked, quashing his embarrassment with a rising irritation at her butting into his life unexpectedly yet again.

She rolled her eyes and put her hands on her hips.

"You do realize that you're always asking me that, right? It's getting kind of rude." She smiled as she said it though, and his heart returned to a semi-regular rhythm. "You could just say hi, like a normal person."

He cleared his throat.

"Hi."

They looked at each other for a moment, Logan's breath hitching at bit as he took in her barely there shorts and tank top. He prayed the push and pull of irritation and attraction wasn't too obvious on his face.

She glanced down at the bottle in his hand.

"Is it a lot of work, cleaning houses?" she asked, a hand twirling around her sleek ponytail.

He shrugged and turned slightly, so he could keep working on the table without the distraction of her eyes on him. The staging was already set up in this room, and a massive dining room table sat covered in dust. He didn't know why someone would move furniture in before the builders were done, but he wasn't here to ask questions. Just clean up.

"It's okay. I've always been pretty tidy. I like things being clean." He bent over the table, gripping the rag a little tighter as he brushed it across the dark mahogany.

She made a "ugh" noise and he turned his head to see her wrinkling her nose.

"You like cleaning?"

"I didn't say that." He moved to a chair, concentrating on a smudge to avoid her eyes. "I like things being clean. Orderly. It's a pain to get it that way, but I do like the sense of accomplishment once it's all over, though."

She didn't say anything, and just watched him work for a moment.

"Can I help?"

"I'm sorry, what?" Logan turned, to see if she was making fun of him. Her face was totally serious. She shrugged.

"My dad has three other houses to look at on this street. I don't want to just stand around."

"Why'd you come with him then?" Logan grimaced. He sounded more irritated than he really felt. It was kind of nice to have someone here to talk to while he worked.

Another shrug.

"He asked me to tag along. I didn't have anything else to do."

"No Spencer or Marissa?"

A dark look settled on her face.

"No."

The word lay heavy between them. He ached to ask her more, but it wasn't his place.

Was it?

"So are you just going to stand there watching, or do you want to help?" he said, giving in to her odd request.

Her face lit up.

"You really want me to help?" She clapped her hands and bounced on her heels.

"Uh, have you ever cleaned anything before?" He narrowed his eyes and frowned. It wouldn't do him any good spending time with her if it meant taking twice as long to clean up after her.

She rolled her eyes.

"Of course."

He bit his lip.

"I mean, like, really cleaned? Gotten down on your hands and knees and scrubbed a toilet?"

"Well, no." She flushed and looked down at her hands. "Maybe I could start with sweeping or something?"

He laughed and went to grab a broom from the supplies by the front door, passing by some of his colleagues to get there. Two were college kids, new this summer, and they didn't talk to Logan much. The older ladies that he'd worked with for the past two summers, however, raised their eyebrows at him as he walked by with broom in hand. His face grew hot under their amused smirks; he knew he'd have to deal with their questions later.

"Let's get started," he said, handing the broom to her. She took it and turned it upside down so the bristles faced the ceiling.

"Like this?" She gave him a quirky half smile that made him forget for a minute he was covered in dust and dirt. He laughed and she giggled, her eyes shining.

They spent most of the next half hour laughing, with Cassie pretending to misunderstand every single direction Logan gave her. He'd tell her to wipe something down, and she'd throw the rag in the air asking 'Like this?' with a dopey grin on her face. Or when he told her to pass him a paper towel, she'd hand him the toilet paper instead. She was careful to not actually make anything messier, or make his job harder; she just made the whole thing more fun.

"You're not like I thought you'd be," he said, watching her wipe a mirror with a cloth.

"What's that supposed to mean?" She turned to face him, hand still wiping.

Logan looked down.

"I meant it as a compliment," he said, not looking at her. He suddenly felt very shy, despite the past half hour of confidently giving her directions. It had been nice knowing something she didn't, even if was just how to properly wipe glass without making streaks. "You're really funny."

"Thanks," she said, her voice soft. He peeked up at her. She had that little half smile on her face again.

"Cass, you don't need to do that." A deep voice behind Logan made his back shoot up straight and Cassie's face pucker.

"Dad! I didn't see you there." She hopped off the stool and flushed. "This is Logan...Hanes."

Heart beating wildly, Logan turned to face the large man in the doorway. He didn't look much like Cassie. His hair was dark with streaks of gray and his wide shoulders took up nearly the entire doorway. A phone in his hand held most of his attention, but he looked up and took Logan in with a quick sweep of his eyes. Logan stood perfectly still, painfully aware of his dirty jeans and dusty t-shirt.

"You did a nice job on this house. Thanks."

Logan let out the breath he'd been holding with a whoosh. He bobbed his head in thanks, and Cassie's dad turned to leave.

"It's time to go Cass," he called over his shoulder, not looking back.

Cassie ran after him without a word to Logan.

Logan stood there for a moment, holding the cloth Cassie had shoved into his hands in her rush to leave.

He felt like the wind had been knocked out of him, and he wasn't sure why. Was it the sudden ditching? The unexpected meeting with her father? He shook his head. Cleaning houses together for a few minutes didn't change anything. She was just someone to talk to about Columbia and New York.

So why was his heart squeezed so tightly in his chest?

A buzz from his phone jerked him out of a spiral into extreme moodiness.

Sorry about that! My dad is not someone you say no to.

Logan breathed a sigh of relief. He could definitely understand that. He sent off a reply before he could think too hard about it.

Too bad. You were really showing promise there as a potential assistant cleaner.

He was pleased at how cool he managed to come off in his messages with her. If only he could be like that when she was actually around him.

Maybe tomorrow could be the next lesson?

He stared at the phone, reading three times to make sure he understood.

You really want to spend all day cleaning with me tomorrow? he asked.

Well… no, came her quick reply.

His fleeting hope vanished like a puff of dust.

But I can drive you. She added a smiley face to the end of the message.

It didn't seem real that someone like Cassie would actually want to hang out with him. But then he remembered the Columbia thing and that the only reason she'd have anything to do with him was because of school.

I do have a few more questions about New York, if that's okay?

There. This way she knew he wasn't interested and it wouldn't be awkward for her. He worried he'd come on a little strong with his comment on her being funny. He could practically see Hideki rolling his eyes at that one.

Of course! That's what I'm here for. See you tomorrow.

Logan suddenly couldn't wait to clean houses again.

CHAPTER THIRTEEN

"FINALLY!" Cassie squealed as her big sister stepped out of the car with their mom. She ran out the front door, still emitting a high pitched noise of excitement and ran to give Diana a hug.

With less than a week to go before the Fourth of July, Cassie had been worried that her mom and sister wouldn't actually come. Even the night before, Di had ignored her beseeching texts demanding to know their arrival time.

"Are you that bored you're excited to see your dull lawyer big sister?"

"You have no idea," said Cassie, pulling out of the hug with a huge sigh. "Dad makes me watch baseball while we eat dinner."

Di widened her eyes and pulled down her open mouth in mock horror.

"Not baseball! What a barbarian. I bet it was all frozen dinners, too?"

"Di, it's been terrible." Cassie linked arms with her sister and walked her into the house. They left her bags in the car, knowing that someone would be along soon to take them in. Along with their mom, some of their staff had arrived to start the preparations for the party. Cassie had enjoyed the break from the constant commotion of a house full of people and staff, but it would be nice to finally eat properly and not have to remind her father to buy food.

As they passed by the head maid, however, Cassie stopped to ask that they not clean her room anymore. The gray-haired woman nodded without comment.

Di, however, had a lot to say about that.

"What's this? You've finally learned to clean up after yourself?" Di raised an eyebrow.

Cassie flushed.

"Well there's no maid at Columbia, is there?"

"True. Wait, does that mean you've finally decided?"

"I guess so..." Cassie trailed off as they walked into the living room. The sun was pouring in through the wide wall of windows, but the house had never seemed this bright until today. Having her whole family together made all the difference in how the house felt.

"Does that mean there's still time to convince you that the west coast and Cali boys are the way to go?" Di wiggled her eyebrows and Cassie giggled.

"That does sound tempting. Anything would be better than Montana boys." Cassie ignored the image of Logan laughing while she swept floors yesterday, as a little voice inside her whispered 'not all Montana boys.'

"Uh oh. What did Spencer do now?"

Cassie hesitated, a lump forming in her throat as she considered how to reply. Her dad hadn't questioned her about where she was going when she'd driven Logan to work the past few days, still assuming she was with Spencer. Everyone still assumed this, since Cassie still hadn't mentioned the breakup to anyone. What would she tell them in a few days when he most definitely did not make an appearance at their party? What if he showed up with Marissa instead?

She told herself this was what she'd wanted. This was her life to live. Her parents didn't decide who she dated, any more than they decided where she went to school…even if they kind of already had.

"We broke up," Cassie said firmly, swallowing the lump in her throat once and for all. Di dropped onto the couch, open-mouthed.

"Wow! Looks like California it is, then!"

A buzz from her phone drew Cassie's attention. She smiled when she saw the name.

"Uh oh, maybe not." Di leaned forward and snagged the phone. "Whoever could be making you so smiley if not the charming Mr. Huntington?"

Cassie made a squawk of annoyance and grabbed for her phone.

Di held it high above her head as looked at the name with her brows furrowed.

"Logan Hanes?" She raised an eyebrow at Cassie.

"Does everyone know him?" Cassie let out a frustrated sigh. "Is he like, secretly famous or something?"

Di shook her head, handing Cassie back her phone.

"It's nothing, just the Hanes name seems familiar. Does he have an older brother I may have dated?"

Cassie laughed.

"No, but way to rub it in my face that you were more popular than me."

Di shrugged.

"I can't help it if I'm the pretty one." She fanned herself with a hand, leaning back in a model's posture to let her long blond hair tumble out artfully behind her. They were practically clones of each other and both plenty beautiful. Cassie knew it, but five years made a big difference. She could still remember sitting on her sister's bed as a gawky ten-year-old watching Di get ready for dates. A different guy every Friday, it seemed like. Now she claimed she was too busy between law school and internships for a boyfriend. If their mom didn't get her fill of harping on Cassie about colleges tonight at dinner, she'd turn on Di to start offering suggestions on finding an eligible bachelor to bring home for dinner.

"But seriously, Cass," Di sat up and crossed one leg over the other, leaning on the armrest to stare at her. "Is this something serious?"

"Oh, my gosh, no!" Cassie screeched, looking around to make sure no one was in the room. "It's just a thing for Columbia. He's going there in the fall and it's a new student match thing. We're just talking about New York and classes and stuff."

Di pursed her lips and stared at Cassie.

"Fine," she said, brushing her hair over her shoulder. It was most definitely not 'fine' but Cassie appreciated her sister being willing to move on to other topics. "So what's the deal with Spencer?"

Relieved to finally have someone to talk to about everything, Cassie launched into a long explanation of all the pressure Spencer had been putting on her and what a jerk he'd been at the restaurant, but left out the fact that Logan had been the waiter. That really wasn't the important part, but how Spencer had treated her after. When she got to the revelation about something happening between the Harts and the Huntingtons, Di frowned.

"Do you know what it's about?" Cassie asked, eying her sister carefully. Di was usually pretty good at hiding her emotions, being the future lawyer and all. But she looked distinctly troubled.

"What did dad say when you asked him?" Di asked, her eyes not quite meeting Cassie's.

"Just that it was a business thing. He said Mr. Huntington introduced him to some business contacts."

"Hmm," was all Di said.

Cassie waited to see if there was more. When her sister remained silent, she decided to just let it drop. Spencer was out of the picture, she still hadn't talked to Marissa since that night, and she was thinking about Logan more than she really wanted to. Her promise to her dad about helping Logan had not involved daydreaming about his dimpled smile and the way his eyes had lit up when he got into her car that morning. She had enough to worry about without adding whatever drama her dad and Spencer's dad had going on.

"Tell me about what's going on in California," Cassie said, though she'd already been out to visit her over spring break. Her sister's life seemed so glamorous, and her friends all very sophisticated. She studied like crazy but at night they'd been out to restaurants and gone sightseeing all weekend.

"Are you really considering it?"

"Considering what?" Their mom's voice rang out from the other side of the room. She'd just walked in from the backyard, where people were measuring for the tents and the landscapers were getting things into shape. The two sisters turned to look at their mother, a third perfect blonde clone without even so much as a wrinkle on her surgically-enhanced forehead. In her pastel pink skirt suit, their mom was like a life-size version of 'Charity Planner Barbie.' Meanwhile, Di was in a pair of cutoffs and an oversized Stanford tank top. Cassie's look was a mirror image of her sister's, though she knew Di had a closet full of skirt suits just like their mom. Cassie got a brief flash of herself in a similar suit, parading through the streets of Los Angeles...and then it shifted to Manhattan. And she wasn't walking alone.

"She's considering joining me in California," said Di, not trying to hide the giddiness in her voice. "Stanford, here she comes!"

Their mom raised an eyebrow and walked over to sit on the chair facing them on the couch.

"I thought we'd agreed on Columbia?"

"I don't..." Cassie looked back and forth between her mom and her sister, both with wide eyes as they waited for her answer. She put her hands under her legs, and took a deep breath. "Do I really need to decide right this second?"

The two women leaned back in their seats and sighed.

"You should have decided months ago," said her mom. "At this rate we'll need to find you an apartment since the dorms will be full, no matter where you choose. That will get expensive."

Cassie's forehead crinkled as she took in this odd comment. This was the first time she'd heard her mother worry about the cost of anything.

"Can we wait until after the party?" Cassie was hoping by then she'd be done with helping Logan and could spend some time thinking about what she wanted in the fall.

"Fine," her mother said in the tone that meant it wasn't fine but she was done talking about it. "Speaking of the party, the Huntingtons haven't RSVP'd yet. Has Spencer said anything to you?"

Cassie looked to her sister, who was studying her nails. Di wouldn't tell her secret, but now that it was out in the world, it seemed pointless to keep it quiet any longer.

"I wouldn't know, I haven't talked to him in days," Cassie said. She took a deep breath. What's the worst that could happen? "We broke up."

Apparently, the worst turned out to be a two-hour fight.

CHAPTER FOURTEEN

EVERY DAY since Logan had given Cassie a cleaning lesson, she'd driven him to work in the morning, and then to the restaurant at night. The first few days he'd been quiet, unused to spending so much time with anyone other than Hideki and his family. But once he started asking questions, it was hard to stop. It was incredible to hear so much about New York, but he felt guilty for taking so much of her time.

"I'm sure you have other things to do this summer," he said on the third day of their new routine.

"Like keg parties?" She arched a brow at him. She was wearing the same cutoffs from the night she'd stopped on the side of the road.

Not that he noticed stuff like that.

"Seriously though," he pressed her a bit. "I want to be sure I'm not keeping you from anything. I don't think this is what Columbia had in mind when they matched me with your dad."

She waved a hand.

"It's helping me too."

He frowned.

"How?"

She gave him a half smile, the one that he'd picture some-times right before he fell asleep at night.

"It's a nice break from all the keggers."

He hadn't asked her that again, but there were plenty of other questions he had for her. Eventually he did run out of New York topics and they made their way into the getting-to-know-each-other kinds of questions that he'd been so hesitant to ask. Surprisingly, she was more than willing to open up. And even more surprisingly, Logan found out they had a lot of stuff in common.

"Favorite food?" he asked.

"Macaroni and cheese."

Excellent choice.

"Coffee or tea?"

"Tea. Coffee is so gross."

Agreed.

"Favorite movie?"

"*Nick and Nora's Infinite Playlist.*"

"Shut up, no it's not." His mouth popped open. It just wasn't possible.

"It totally is! Why? Is that weird?" Her brows scrunched up, and she twisted her mouth into a little frown. He'd noticed himself staring at her mouth more and more during the rapid fire questioning session in the short drive to the restaurant.

"It's just...that's my favorite, too," he said as heat crept up his neck and into his cheeks. "It's the one that made me want to go live in New York one day."

She pulled into the parking lot of the restaurant and turned to smile at him. Her eyes were sparkling.

"It made me want to live in New York, too."

He messed up five drink orders that night and had to give up a fair chunk of his tips to keep his coworkers happy, but he just couldn't get the picture of him and Cassie in New York out of his mind.

It was stupid, he told himself. Just because they both liked mac n' cheese and a random movie, that didn't mean anything.

Did it?

ONE NIGHT, just a few days before the Fourth of July, Cassie showed up after Logan's shift at the restaurant. Hideki was already there waiting for him, and when they saw Cassie get out of her car, his cousin let out a low whistle.

"Seriously, shut up, Hideki," Logan hissed at him. Cassie spotted them and waved Logan over, but he stayed put. "I don't want to go with her."

"Why not? Pretty sure riding around in cars at night with hot cheerleaders is key to the best summer ever. Even if it's not technically on the BSE list."

"I smell like the restaurant, that's why!" Logan flushed. He knew his cousin had noticed all the extra time he was spending getting ready for his shifts now. Even his aunt had commented once or twice on the sudden increase in gel and cologne usage. Logan knew it wouldn't make much of a difference—he could never compare to someone like Spencer—but he was still hoping to erase that very first impression he'd made on her, dirty and broken on the side of the road.

Hideki called out to Cassie across the parking lot.

"He says he stinks! Maybe next time?"

Cassie threw up her hands and marched over. It was the same look she'd had when forcing him to go to the doctor. Logan wasn't sure why he even bothered resisting at this point.

"Come on, let's go to the lake," she said when she was within hearing distance. She looked at Hideki and smiled, though her eyes looked moist with recently dried tears. "You coming with us, Hideki?"

"Dude, she remembered my name," he said in a stage whisper. "And even said it right."

Logan closed his eyes and wished he were anywhere else in the world.

"No thanks, I had to pause a seriously intense game of *Madden* to come out here. He's all yours."

Logan's face grew hot and he took a deep breath to stop himself from punching his cousin in front of Cassie.

"Let's go," she said, and grabbed Logan's hand. She practically dragged him over to her car.

"Woah, what's up?" He tried to ignore the tingling in his hand and focused on her frown.

"Nothing, just family stuff. I don't want to be at home right now."

Logan's eyebrows drew together. They'd never gotten this personal before in their conversations, beyond the recent revelation of their shared love of New York movies. And that time she mentioned her first kiss in Bryant Park.

Not that he still thought about that.

"Wouldn't you rather be with Spencer or Marissa?"

"We broke up, okay?" She dropped his hand and turned to face him. Her angry eyes softened when she saw Logan's open mouthed surprise. "Sorry, it's just part of all the family drama tonight. We broke up that night we were at the restaurant, and I only told my parents tonight. They were not happy about it."

She unlocked the car and opened her door with a frustrated huff. Logan walked slowly to the other side, slightly regretting now not going home with Hideki. This was not what he'd expected to be doing tonight and he didn't like feeling unprepared.

He thought about everything he'd said and done in the past

few weeks. She hadn't been with Spencer nearly the whole time she'd been spending time with him. Did that mean something?

Logan sat in silence as she maneuvered out of the parking lot, wracking his brain for how best to respond to the bombshell news. Hopefully better than her parents had.

"Why does it matter to your parents that you guys broke up?"

She shook her head.

"There's a big party they throw every year on the Fourth of July. The Huntingtons usually come, and a lot of other people. They're worried this year they won't show, and it'll be bad for Dad's business. He gets a lot of clients from Mitch Huntington."

This was completely beyond the world Logan knew about, he didn't think anything he could say would help.

"That sucks," was all he could come up with. Cassie shot him a grateful smile and his heart fluttered.

"The whole time I was with Spencer, I felt like it was just to make my parents happy. They didn't even care that I didn't like him that much or that he was such a jerk. It was what was expected of me, you know?"

Logan shook his head.

"Not really, no. No one ever expected much from me."

Cassie sighed wistfully.

"That must be nice. Having a blank canvas like that."

"I'd never thought about it that way. I'd rather be known for something bad than not known at all."

Cassie didn't respond. They pulled into a parking lot near one of the rockier beaches. It was deserted at this time of night. They got out into the cool midsummer air, and Logan breathed in the sharp tang of the lake. The days were still hot, but nights could get chilly. He noticed Cassie shivering a little in just her shorts and a long sleeved shirt. He shrugged off his jacket and held it out to her.

"Here," he said. "You need this more than me."

She looked up at him, and he was surprised to see tears in her eyes. Surprised and slightly panicked.

"I'm sorry!" He pulled his jacket back to his chest. "I don't... I don't know what to do here. I don't have a lot of friends. Girls. Girlfriends. I mean, friends who are girls."

Great, now he was babbling, and she was crying. He could hear Hideki laughing already.

"No, I'm sorry." She sniffed and wiped her nose on her sleeve and sat down on the large rock at the water's edge. "It's just the first time tonight someone has thought about what I need or want."

Logan felt his heart start to speed up. He'd actually done something right! Something helpful. He felt so much in her debt sometimes, with everything she was doing to help him, it felt good to know he could help her, too.

He walked over to her and placed the jacket on her shoulders.

"Is there anything else you need right now?" he asked softly, standing as close to her as he dared. Close enough to catch a whiff of her fruity shampoo as a light breeze whipped past and blew her hair back. The water on the lake was bright, and she'd left the headlights of the car on so they could see their way down to the shore. Their shadows loomed high and blended together in the water.

"You could sit here and talk to me about something totally random to help me forget."

Logan nodded.

"I think I can do that." He sat down next to her on the rock, keeping a good twelve inches between them. This was not the moment to try anything other than jacket lending, as much as his brain was screaming for him to go for it. "Do you want to know why my middle name is Cousteau?"

She let out a short laugh.

"I have been wondering, ever since the doctor's office."

He flushed. Why was he telling her this? No one knew this. But she asked for something random.

"I'm born on the day Jacques Cousteau died. My mom didn't know what to give me as a middle name, and it was all over the news that day."

"What?" She turned to look at him, her eyes sparkling with leftover tears in the moonlight.

"He's this French ocean—"

"I know who he is," she interrupted, her face scrunched up yet still perfect and beautiful. "I forgot you're a Cancer. Water sign. Makes sense now."

He raised an eyebrow. He wasn't sure if he was more surprised that she knew who Jacques Cousteau was or that she was into astrology. This was a night for surprises, apparently.

"You know Cousteau?"

She shrugged.

"My dad was really into him. It's unavoidable really."

"What do you mean by 'really into him'?" Logan narrowed his eyes. "This is not like being into comic books or Star Wars or something mainstream geeky. This is science geeky stuff." Her dad was a big shot real estate developer. Not exactly the typical type to like this kind of stuff.

Cassie sighed and leaned back on her hands, looking out into the shimmering darkness of the lake.

"Well, you know how everyone has their one thing?"

Logan shook his head.

"You know." She turned to look at him, her eyes wide. "Everyone has one random silly thing that they love and can't explain. There's no reason. It's just part of you. His is a Cousteau obsession."

Logan leaned back as well and considered this. What did he randomly love?

"So mine is Cousteau, too?"

Logan wasn't sure he liked having something in common with her father. He hadn't been super impressed with what he'd seen at the house he'd been cleaning. Just intimidated. And to hear that he'd cared more about his daughter being with a guy to help his business than her feelings didn't exactly made him sound great.

Plus there was the lingering question Logan still had to ask his mom. Why she was so against the Harts? He tried to remember back to when his mom had been working for him, but nothing came to mind. It had been over a year ago, and right now, sitting on a rock by the lake next to Cassie, he didn't really want to think about his mom.

Especially since Cassie was now watching him carefully with her very green and very distracting eyes. He shifted a little. The rock was not the most comfortable seat but if she wasn't bothered, neither was he.

"No, you're not obsessed with Cousteau, not like he is. Hello, he named his daughter Calypso for crying out loud."

Logan turned to look at her, his mouth dropping open.

"I didn't know that was your full name."

She reached up to brush her long hair in front her face that was turning a beet red. He cringed.

Way to make her feel even worse tonight.

"You don't go by Callie instead?" He tried desperately to make up for his rudeness.

She shrugged.

"It's something my sister started. She's named Diane, like Cousteau's daughter."

"Wow, he really is obsessed."

Cassie laughed.

"Yeah, it seems to have faded a bit with time. Now he just fishes mostly."

"Sorry, I didn't mean to talk so much about your dad when you're so mad at him," Logan said, his stomach sinking when he realized that this was probably not what she'd needed.

"No, it's fine, it's helping."

Logan raised an eyebrow. She giggled.

"Really. He's not a bad guy. It's good to remember his little quirks. I try so hard to make him proud, I forget he's a real person, too."

Logan nodded.

"I kind of get that. That's why I'm so amped about Columbia. My mom is so freaking proud. It feels awesome."

"So it's just you and your mom?"

Logan nodded and frowned. She'd shared a lot with him, but he wasn't sure he was ready to share this. Not even Hideki asked about his dad, not anymore.

Neither said anything for a few minutes and they just looked out at the water. The gentle lapping against the shore was soothing...but also kind of romantic. Logan shifted a little in his seat, moving two inches closer to Cassie.

"Thanks for talking with me tonight," she said, standing up. She handed back his jacket and the breath whooshed out of Logan's chest. "I hope you won't get in trouble with your aunt for being out so late."

Logan couldn't help but laugh.

"Please, she'd be thrilled to know I'm out with a—" He stopped himself and blushed a deep scarlet. "I mean, she won't care."

Cassie had that half-smile on her face that did funny things to Logan's stomach, but she didn't say anything. After long awkward minute of Logan's mind racing as he thought of something else to say, she made her way to the car. He let out a long breath and followed her.

When she dropped him off, he didn't go in right away. He stood on the porch and watched her drive away.

Cassie Hart was nothing like he'd expected but she also represented everything he wasn't. She was part of a world he hated and she was forced into pretending to like it. He didn't think she hated it though. But tonight something had shifted, and he'd seen a glimpse of what it would be like to be a part of that world. A part of her world.

Was he ready for that?

CHAPTER FIFTEEN

THE DAYS before the Fourth of July party were not as fun as they had been in previous years for Cassie. Her sister was happy to go out and walk around town with her, but her parents were barely looking at her and speaking in forced polite tones. Even telling them she'd decided on Columbia didn't make a difference.

"Well, thank goodness you've come to your senses," was all her mother said. "We need everything settled as soon as possible before..."

Her mom trailed off and looked up at her dad. They were all sitting at the breakfast table eating waffles the housekeeper had prepared.

"Before the end of summer," her mom finished and changed the subject to finalizing the flowers for the backyard.

The bright spot in her days were the drives with Logan. After the night at the lake, she had to admit to her herself that she was at least crushing on him a little. There was no other explanation for the eagerness she felt when she got a message from him or the excited flutter in her stomach when she saw his face light up when she pulled up to his house.

She actually even started a message to Marissa, asking her if it was too soon after Spencer to think about someone else, and if she was crazy for even considering Logan. He was from a completely different world and was the total opposite of what her parents wanted. Besides, he didn't even like her that much. He was just putting up with her because he wanted to hear about New York.

And yet...he'd been so sweet when she was crying the other night, maybe he didn't think she was totally terrible. Then she'd remember what she'd done to him and that she *was* terrible. This crush had to stay under control. So what if her heart skipped a beat on those rare occasions his dimpled smile made an appearance? It wasn't going to happen, for so many reasons.

Cassie really needed the advice of a best friend.

But in the end, she deleted the message. It had been weeks, and no word from Marissa. Why should Cassie reach out first? She hadn't been the one to pick a boy over her best friend.

There was still no word if the Huntingtons were coming to the party. If Spencer came, would Marissa be with him? Cassie was not looking forward to a potential showdown in front of her family.

On the morning of the party, Cassie still hadn't decided if she should reach out to Marissa, just to see once and for all if she would be there that night. Her sister had proved completely unhelpful in giving advice, saying simply that if they showed and Cassie wanted to bail, then she'd cover for her.

Until that moment, Cassie hadn't even considered not going as an option. It was the one thing the family did together every summer. Her mom planned her charity events around it, and her dad took off work. He'd taken off a lot more than usual this summer to be with Cassie, but still, it seemed like abandoning her family if she didn't go.

All it took was seeing the Huntington's car pull up, however, and Spencer step out with Marissa on his arm for Cassie to quickly take her sister up on her offer. The look on Marissa's face was one of pure joy, and Cassie felt sick to her stomach as Spencer wrapped his arm around her waist.

"I'm out of here," she whispered to Di as Spencer and Marissa made their way from the house into the backyard. The view facing the lake was one of the best to see the fireworks, and it killed her to be missing it. But she was pretty sure that being here would kill her more.

It wasn't like she cared that Spencer was with someone else. It was the disappointment in her parents' eyes that she wanted to escape. Her irritation with Marissa paled in comparison to that.

Cassie made her way along the side of the yard past the dozen or so guests who were already there, and snuck around to the front of the house. She groaned when she realized her car was blocked in by all the others. This was not going to be easy.

She was dressed in wedges and a summer dress, not exactly fit for walking anywhere. It wasn't even really fit for the cool evening air, but she hadn't realized quite how chilly it was under the heat lamps in the backyard. She didn't want to risk going back in the house to get a jacket and someone seeing her. There was only one person she wanted to see right now, and he didn't have a car. She bit her lip, considering her options...

Hey what are you doing tonight?

She held her breath as she waited for Logan's answer, which came almost instantly.

Just hanging out with my family.

Cassie took a deep breath before hitting send on her next message.

Do you think your cousin would mind if you guys came and got me?

It was a big ask. He owed her nothing, and she didn't deserve his help. But hope flickered as the blinking dots appeared in the messenger window, telling her he was typing. Her heart pounded as she waited for a response.

We'll be there in 10.

CASSIE WAS SUDDENLY VERY shy as she walked into Logan's aunt and uncle's house. They were all sitting around a table, playing a board game.

"What a nice surprise to see one of Logan's friends!" His aunt gave her a wide smile. Cassie flushed. Friends. That's all they were. That's all he wanted them to be. "Care to join us for a game? We don't head down to the lake until a little after 9."

"We like to keep things pretty low key," his uncle added with a joking grin that looked just like Hideki's.

Cassie felt a wave of relief wash over her.

"Low key sounds great," she said. "Sorry for interrupting your evening."

"It's fine. We're happy to meet one of Logan's friends from school. And how exciting you'll both be going to Columbia in the fall! It's great they were able to match you up so he could hear more about it."

Cassie shot a look at Logan, whose cheeks were tinged with red. He'd apparently talked about her to his family quite a bit more than she'd talked to hers. Of course, he had no reason to hide it, unlike her.

Logan cleared his throat.

"Is it okay if I leave the game? I thought we might head down to the lake early. Get a good spot."

His aunt and uncle exchanged glances before nodding, but Hideki was less discreet and grinned like a jack-o-lantern.

Logan took Cassie by the arm and led her back towards the door before his cousin could open his mouth.

"It was nice to meet you!" she called back over her shoulder. Logan stopped to grab a jacket from the hall closet and one of the beach bags full of blankets by the door and they were back out in the cool night. He placed the jacket on her bare shoulders and slung the bag over his shoulder.

"It's almost two miles down to the park, actually," he said, looking down at her shoes. "When we were younger we'd take our bikes and spend the whole day out there, but the past few summers we've been working and this year with my shoulder—"

"I can handle a short walk," she said, lifting her chin. She felt the familiar twinge of guilt in her stomach when he mentioned his shoulder. He didn't talk about it that often, but every single time he did she wondered how his summer would have been without the accident.

"Sorry I ruined your evening with your family," she said, pulling the jacket around her. It was the same one from that night at the lake and the smell of him overwhelmed her senses— fresh and citrusy, but also with hints of spices. Ginger, maybe. His whole house had smelled delicious.

"Hideki can get super intense with games," Logan said with a chuckle. "Trust me, you made things a lot better."

Was he talking about just tonight? Her heart fluttered.

They walked in silence for a while. Cassie looked up at the sky.

"I'll miss the quiet in New York," she said, trying to get a hold of her emotions. This was just like driving him around. Except it was nothing like that. "And the stars."

Logan smiled and her stomach did a backflip at the sight of his dimple.

"I think about that all the time," he said softly. "How far away from quiet I'll be."

She looked at his floppy hair falling across his forehead and the look of pure attentiveness in his eyes. The tiny crush she'd been telling herself wasn't really there suddenly burst into full bloom. She almost stopped walking, the feeling was so overwhelming.

He was so different than everyone else in her life. No phony front, no pretending to be someone he wasn't. He liked things clean, and calm, and quiet. He hated the world she came from; she'd known that since that first night. He wouldn't even be talking to her if he didn't want to hear about Columbia. When the summer was over, they'd both go off to New York and he'd have his friends while she kept doing what she did best—making her parents happy. She'd major in business and help her dad during the summers. She'd meet someone else just like Spencer but from an even bigger family and make her mother delirious with joy when she brought him home over winter break. It was all so clearly laid out before her.

"I want to major in art history," she said in a rush, her face growing hot. There, she'd finally said it out loud. "My parents want me to major in business or pre-law or something useful. But I like art."

He smiled.

That damn dimple.

"What's your favorite museum?"

"Definitely the Met. A boring choice, I know, but they have everything." She started to babble. This blooming crush was turning her into her most awkward self. Like, middle school awkward. "I can spend a whole day in just one little section. And it's right on Central Park so you can go right out into nature instead of into the city."

"Will you take me?" he said softly, as if he was afraid of her answer. As if she'd ever be able to deny him something. "When we're in New York?"

Her heart started to beat faster and her feet picked up the pace as well. She needed to sit down all of a sudden.

"You want me to take you to an art museum? Do you even like art?"

"I'd like it with you."

Just then, they rounded a corner and a voice called out to Logan, saving her from needing to examine the flood of emotions his response had given her. A big group of people was making their way down to the lake and Logan greeted them all by name while Cassie stood by and waved a silent hello. They were all from the restaurant, she gathered, from the way they were talking.

Cassie walked along slightly behind Logan, listening to him joke around with the others. They all liked him, she could tell. And why wouldn't they? He was funny and thoughtful and apparently wanted to go to art museums. With her.

As a group they made their way into the park. Logan laid out the blankets in a spot a little further back than the others, however. They were right against the trees and could see the expanse of the lake stretching out before them. As the show got started, she saw the edges of the lake dotted with boats lit up in the night sky.

"So your thing is art?" Logan said, his arms wrapped around his knees, his golden hair tinged green in the light of the fireworks.

"My thing?"

"You know, you said everyone has that one thing they like."

"Ah yes, Monsieur Cousteau," she giggled, but nervously, not as cute as she would have liked. Was his heart not racing the way hers was? "Though art is a pretty normal thing to like. I like Claude Cahun. Not everyone does. But I just do."

"I haven't heard of him."

"Her." Logan flushed. "Most people haven't," she rushed to

explain. "Don't be embarrassed. It's not like her stuff is taught in schools. She was a little out there."

He put his chin on his knees and looked at her, his eyes catching some of the blue from the fireworks.

"Mine's hammerheads."

"What?" With the booming overhead, she wasn't sure she'd heard him correctly.

He cleared his throat.

"I just...I saw this documentary about hammerheads when I was little. My parents did kind of push the ocean stuff a little, just because of my name. The only thing that ever stuck though was hammerhead sharks."

"Why?" It was a little odd, but seemed so very Logan. She thought of his profile picture.

He shrugged. Another very Logan thing he did. He would purse his lips right before he did it. And a very large percentage of her attention was on his lips right now.

"They do this mating dance." He flushed and looked down. "I was little, I didn't know what that was. I just remember seeing hundreds of them swimming around each other, dancing. I saw these giant powerful things, but also beautiful."

"Like you," Cassie whispered, and she bit her lip. *What a ridiculous thing to say.*

Logan looked up at her.

"No, like you."

She could feel her entire body leaning toward him, but he stayed curled up against his knees, until another firework burst in the sky and he jerked up, placing his hands behind him and scooting ever so slowly closer to her.

With the sound of the fireworks booming overhead, Cassie could only feel the pounding of her heart instead of hear it. She had never felt this kind of giddiness around Spencer, not even in the very first weeks of dating. There were mere inches of space between her and Logan, and every part of her body was electrified by his presence.

Slowly, softly, his hand slid on top of hers where it rested between them on the blanket. She tucked her head slightly and turned to look at him. He was staring up at the fireworks, his face bathed in blue and red, his eyes wide. He looked half-impressed and half-terrified.

In that moment, she realized he'd never done this before. Her first instinct was to tease him, as she'd been doing all summer.

Instead, she leaned her head toward his ear, making sure to keep her hand underneath his.

"Do you like the show?" she said, a little louder than normal to make sure he could hear her over the noise.

"It's great!" he yelled back, then turned his head quickly.

For a brief second their noses touched, their eyes open and staring. Cassie inhaled sharply at the tenderness and sincerity she saw in his deep brown swirls. This close, she could hear his breath coming in short, ragged bursts. When she couldn't stand his piercing gaze anymore, she closed her eyes, and leaned in the tiniest bit to let him know this was what she wanted.

She'd never wanted anything more.

The softest kiss brushed across her lips, and she sighed. She reached up her hand to curl around his neck, and opened her mouth slightly. He pushed forward eagerly, both hands reaching up to cup her face. He tasted like summer and sweetness and everything good. Fireworks burst inside of her twice as big as anything happening in the sky.

This wasn't what she'd expected from this summer at the lake.

It was so much better.

CHAPTER SIXTEEN

SHOULD MY HANDS GO HERE?

Is this okay?

Should I open my mouth more? Or less?

Logan was so nervous he couldn't get his mind to shut off.

Then suddenly Cassie sighed into him and he let himself go.

Everything in his life had been hard up until now, but this was easy. And fun. And freaking amazing.

He was vaguely aware of the fireworks ending when everyone stood up to leave. Cassie pulled away and looked around, her face flushed even in the moonlight.

"Should we head back?" she asked, looking around at the trickle of people walking past.

Was she so eager to get away? His stomach lurched.

"Let's wait for all the cars to clear out." He didn't want to leave. Not yet.

She nodded and settled on her back.

"You can't even see the stars anymore through the smoke." Her voice was soft and low, and something inside him rumbled in response.

He leaned back, slowly, his arm just inches from hers. As soon as he was settled she slipped her hand into his. A warm wave of relief washed over him.

"More like the sky in New York?" he asked, trying to get his heart rate to slow down. It had been on overdrive since the second their lips had touched.

"Hmm," was all she said and turned on her side to face him.

He twisted to look at her but the twinge in his shoulder stopped him. He grimaced and her forehead crinkled.

"Does it still hurt a lot?"

He shook his head. He didn't want to think about that night right now, other than as the night they met. He could never have imagined his life could change so much in such a short amount of time.

When she leaned over to place her hands on either side of his head and landed a gentle kiss on his lips, he reached up to tangle his hands in her hair. Their kisses deepened and the rumble inside of him turned into a roar. He wrapped his arms around her, ignoring the twinge in his shoulder to hold her tightly as their lips crashed into each other again and again.

A lot was hard in his life. He didn't have money, or a car, and had been working two jobs every summer just to be able to save enough to afford the necessities. He didn't know if he'd be able to make it in New York at school, on his own. From everything Cassie had told him, it would be ten times harder to find and keep a job on top of all the schoolwork. Life was always going to be hard for him.

But this...this was easy.

He could have stayed there all night, but a buzz from her bag drew her out of the kiss. He let out a small groan and she gave him that heart-melting half-smile.

Her smile faded the instant she looked at her phone, however.

"I need to get back," she said, standing up. She held out a hand to help him up, but he ignored it, pushing off with his good arm to stand beside her.

He pulled out his phone to call his uncle as she bent to gather the blankets. His uncle was almost home and said he'd come back with the car to pick them up. Logan took Cassie's hand as they walked to the main entrance to the park and joined the long line of people waiting for rides in the parking lot. They stood as close to each other as possible, nose to nose, ignoring the others around them. When she shivered under his jacket, he rubbed her arms.

"I like the way you look in that jacket," he whispered. It was one of his favorite green hoodies, and was three sizes too big for her. She'd rolled up the sleeves to be able to take his hand. She actually looked a little silly. But it was so different than the polished perfection she usually was. And the green made her eyes, already sparkling in the starlight, even more intense.

She flushed, and looked down.

How could anything he say make that impression on her? Had Spencer never complimented her? Didn't she know how incredible she was?

Rather than say everything that was swirling around in his mind, he rested his forehead against hers. He breathed her in, a little thrill running through him when he heard her heart beating just as fast as his.

A honk pulled them out of their embrace. His uncle waved from his truck as is pulled up in front of them.

"I should...ride back alone." Cassie bit her lip.

Logan felt a sharp stab in his heart, before practicality took over. The awkwardness of riding with his uncle was probably a little too much for her—and Logan if he was being honest with himself. He nodded.

When she went to take off the jacket, however, he shook his head.

"Keep it."

She placed the briefest of pecks on his cheek that guaranteed to warm him throughout the entire walk home.

Of all the ways Logan had pictured spending the Fourth of July, making out with Cassie Hart had not been one of them. Not even in the ballpark. Not even in the parking lot of the stadium.

Not that it hadn't been pretty awesome. She was pretty awesome, actually. The rich-girl-cheerleader facade had faded away over the past few weeks and he'd been able to see her as just Cassie. She was funny, and smart, and so different from what he'd pictured. That first night they'd met on the side of the road, she'd been the embodiment of everything he hated. Then it turned out she was bossy, and opinionated, and more worried about appearances than he'd ever been or would be.

But despite everything, he was falling pretty hard, and didn't know how to stop himself.

He wasn't sure he wanted to stop.

CHAPTER SEVENTEEN

DROPPING LOGAN'S jacket in her car as she passed it, Cassie managed to sneak back into the party at her house right as everyone was leaving. Her sister's message had been insistent —***get home NOW, Mom and Dad know you're gone***— but she hadn't expected it to be so hard to leave Logan. Still, she couldn't risk anyone seeing him in the car with her.

She wasn't embarrassed. Far from it. Logan was the sweetest, funniest, most caring guy she'd ever known. And then there was the way he looked at her. No one had ever looked at her like that—like they really saw her for who she was.

No, she wasn't embarrassed. But her family knowing about him could cause both of them so much trouble, and she'd already messed up his life enough.

Once all the adrenaline from what had probably been the world's most perfect first kiss (well, kisses) had left her system, she realized what a mess she was in. She was falling hard for a guy her parents would never approve of. While standing up to them about her college major seemed manageable, them finding out about Logan the same night they'd seen Spencer with his new girlfriend would be much harder to handle. It was not the right time to flaunt a new, much less socially acceptable (to them) guy in front of all of their friends.

As Cassie mingled with the remaining guests, her mother and Di both gave her lingering glances, her sister looking relieved and her mother pissed off. Cassie wanted to avoid any questions for as long as possible so she made her way over to the guest house at the back of the property calling, "I'll make sure it's empty!" to anyone who would listen.

She was actually hoping to hide out there for a while, send a message to Logan to let him know she got back, and relive a few of the sweeter moments of the evening. But she stopped in her tracks as a faint giggling floated out from the guest house. She'd seen her sister so she knew it wasn't her. Mr. and Mrs. Huntington were still at the party, but Spencer was nowhere to be seen amongst the heat lamps and food tables. And no Marissa in the yard, either.

Cassie's blood started to boil as annoyance seeped through her. It was one thing for Marissa to ditch her for a guy she'd just dumped. It was what Cassie had kind of wanted, after all. But to make out with him in Cassie's guest house was a little much. She'd been patient with Marissa, not wanting any friendship drama to stand in the way of her best friend's dream guy, but this was just rude. All the lingering happy feelings from kissing Logan were now totally squashed by the thought of Spencer and Marissa getting busy on her property.

"Party's over, kids!" she called as she pushed open the door to the guest house, irritation coursing through her veins.

She heard a shriek from the loft and caught the flash of a red dress above—the same color Marissa had been wearing. Cassie waited but no one emerged down the steps.

"Spencer, seriously, your parents are leaving. Get dressed and get out of my house."

There was still no answer. If it wasn't Spencer, she was sure the guy would have said something. So it had to be them.

Cassie closed her eyes and took a deep breath. She didn't want to hash it out here. She wanted to remember this night as her first kiss with Logan, not as the night she definitively lost her best friend. The giant fight she knew was coming could wait a little longer.

With an annoyed sigh loud enough for them to hear, she slammed the door and stalked back through the yard to the main house. Her mom stopped her with a hand on her arm, gentle but firm.

"When everyone is gone, you better be ready to tell me where you were," her mom said with a little smile and nod at a few people who were waving goodbye to her. "This was your chance to get Spencer back and you missed it. Now look what he's gotten up to."

Cassie couldn't help herself and looked back to see Spencer and Marissa holding hands as they left the guest house. The few appetizers she'd had hours ago churned in her stomach. Why was it so hard to see them together? They'd arrived at the party together, but she could still tell herself nothing had really happened and maybe they were just there as friends. This was proof that it was something serious.

And something that made her parents extremely unhappy.

Cassie put on her best smile and slid her arm out of her mom's hand. There were still a dozen or so people in the yard, and she could feel every single one of their eyes on her.

"Everything is under control, Mom," she said, keeping her back straight the way she'd been taught. "I'm tired though. Can we talk in the morning?"

Her mom narrowed her eyes but nodded, her cold smile never wavering.

Cassie waited until she was in the house to let out a tiny

grunt of frustration. Di couldn't have covered her for another hour? Then no one would have even known about Spencer and Marissa. Cassie could have lived another few days without picturing the two of them together.

As Cassie walked up to her room, she tried desperately to think of an excuse to tell her mom about why she'd left. Maybe an emergency with a friend? No, everyone they knew was at this party. She felt sick and had walked herself to the hospital? That sounded even less believable...

Her phone buzzed, pulling her out of her troubled thoughts. A message from Logan flashed across the screen.

Thanks for watching the fireworks with me.

A smile rose to her lips, the first since she'd gotten home. Suddenly, things didn't seem quite so bad.

CHAPTER EIGHTEEN

AS LOGAN WALKED in the door to his aunt's house, he was expecting to deal with Hideki's thousand questions about the evening.

He was not expecting to see his mom sitting on the couch, waiting for him.

"Mom! You made it up!" He was so happy to avoid Hideki's curiosity, he didn't stop to think about how odd it was that she was here. Just two days ago she'd told him she'd have to work and couldn't come. "Were you able to see any of the fireworks?"

His mom shook her head.

"Come sit, Logan."

"It's kind of late," he said, yawning and stretching. His shoulder was a little stiff from lying on the ground, but he didn't mind. "You must be wiped out from the drive. Can we talk tomorrow?"

His mom shifted in her seat.

"No, I drove all night because I need you to hear this now. Before anything else happens."

"What happened?"

"You were out with Cassie Hart, weren't you?"

Logan stopped in the middle of another yawn.

"How do you know that?" He dropped his arms and furrowed his brow.

"I called your phone a few times and when I couldn't reach you, I called Caroline. She said you were probably too busy with Cassie to hear your phone."

It's true he'd seen a few missed calls when he'd called his uncle to pick up Cassie. He told himself he'd look at them on the walk home, but his mind had been stuck on Cassie and everything they'd done.

His mom's arched eyebrow told him she knew exactly what they'd been doing. Logan flushed. At least she hadn't gone down to the park to find him. Being caught in the middle of making out with someone by his mom was definitely *not* on the BSE list.

"You drove all the way out here because I was finally on a date with a girl?" He held back a groan. "Weird time to get over-protective when I'm about to move across the country to school."

"Logan, this is serious!" The look she shot him finally made him sit down. Her hands were clasped tightly in her lap.

"Sorry, Mom," he said automatically, as he settled into a seat across from her. She was at her most serious. All he wanted to do was sleep and relive every detail of his night with Cassie, so the sooner he heard whatever his mom wanted to say, the sooner it was over. "What's up?"

"I didn't drive all night because you were on a date," she said with a sigh. "I drove all night because you were with Cassie Hart. I thought it was just something for school."

"It was," said Logan, and flushed again. "And now it's...a little more than that."

Yikes, this was embarrassing. She couldn't have waited two months to become interested in his love life once he was safely 2,000 miles away?

"How much more?" She narrowed her eyes. Logan felt a jolt of panic shoot through him.

"Geez, Mom, I don't know! It's literally a new thing that just started tonight."

His mom let out a breath and leaned back in her seat.

"So it's not that serious, good. You won't break her heart if you break it off," she said. Then, almost to herself, "Though her heart will be broken anyway by all of this..."

"Mom, what are you talking about? Breaking her heart? I don't even know what this is. She's the first girl I've ever, uh, liked like this before." Phew, he avoided letting his mom know he'd never kissed a girl before tonight. Hideki already teased him enough about it, though tonight probably made up for it times a million. He could still remember the feel of her hand on his neck and in his hair as they'd kissed.

"You can't see her anymore, Logan."

"What? Why?" He sat up straight as thoughts of her lips on his vanished in an instant.

His mom ran a hand through her long brown hair. She normally wore it up, very professional looking, but tonight it was draped loosely over her shoulders. She looked both older and younger than she usually did. She'd been so young when she'd had Logan, barely older than he was now.

"It's complicated. Can you please just trust me on this?"

Logan shook his head. Secrets were not usually how they operated. It had been just the two of them for so long, they'd relied on each other too much. She always explained everything she did, so he'd never feel like she was lying. Every question about his dad, no matter how painful, she'd answered. The only person who lied in their family was Logan's dad.

But all summer, his mom had been weird whenever he mentioned Cassie's name. He figured if it was something worth mentioning, she would have already. But, apparently, it was only worth mentioning now that he was actually falling for the girl.

"No, Mom, I need to know."

His mom sighed.

"Fine, but just know I didn't tell you all this because I didn't want to ruin your last summer at home with all this drama."

He waited, his heart racing. The possibilities were endless, and his mind flitted from one improbable scenario to the next.

"You can't be with Cassie because I'm in the middle of suing her father."

Logan blinked and frowned. That had not been one of the scenarios.

"Suing him? For what? You worked for him ages ago, why are you suing him now?"

"Wrongful termination."

He thought about that for a moment.

"I thought you quit that job?"

She shook her head and rubbed her eyes. She looked so tired.

"As soon as I started, the disgusting way they treated their female employees was pretty clear." His mom's voice was hesitant. She didn't want to tell him this. "The jokes they made, the random shoulder touches and brushing back of hair."

She wrapped her arms around herself.

"Sometimes it was more than that. Never with me; I wasn't young enough for their taste apparently. So many of the girls were barely out of college and they didn't say anything to the men when they'd do it. But they'd talk to me about it during breaks. They said it was normal, that's just how guys were, but the pain in their eyes..."

She shook her head and closed her eyes. Logan's hands started to ball into fists. She said they hadn't done anything to her but the thought of any man treating someone like that made him sick to his stomach.

"I tried to get them to say something, but they were all afraid of losing their jobs. At this point in my life, I have way less patience for that kind of misogynistic crap."

An intense urge to hit something bubbled up in Logan, alongside a wave of guilt that he'd had no idea that she'd been dealing with this.

"How did I miss how stressed you were last year?"

She shrugged and shook her head.

"Probably because you were in the middle of your SAT and college application madness," she said with a sad smile. "I didn't want this to distract you."

It was true, he'd barely noticed or thought of anything other than schoolwork and colleges most of junior year.

"So you quit because Mr. Hart was a jerk?" Logan could totally get that. Every boss he'd ever had was a jerk.

"Not exactly." His mom twisted her watch around her wrist. "I went to him and his partner and told them it had to stop. I thought maybe they just didn't realize what they were doing." She shook her head. "It's such a small company, they don't have an HR person on staff. All the other places I worked were really rigorous in their harassment training. I felt like I had to say something."

Logan nodded. This all seemed like such adult things to worry about, but wasn't he technically one now?

"Of course you did. I'm sorry I didn't notice with everything at school—"

She held up a hand.

"Logan, you're a brilliant and caring young man, but I still like to protect you when I can. Like I said, I didn't want you worrying about any of this."

Of course she didn't. All she'd ever done was worry about him. Whose job was it to worry about her?

"So the wrongful termination...he fired you when you complained?"

She shook her head.

"No, he got really upset. They told me that I'd never be able to find work anywhere in Helena if I didn't quit right then and keep my mouth shut. I wasn't expecting that." She blinked back tears. "But with you going off to school soon, I didn't want to find myself without the ability to get a new job, so I quit."

Logan's heart sank. She'd sacrificed so much for him over the years, making sure he could go to the best private school in Helena, going without what she needed so he could have a chance at better things. And this was what she got in return? He stood up and went to fold her into a hug, towering over her. She sniffed as a few tears started to fall.

"I tried to put it out of my mind and get on with another job, but I couldn't stop thinking about it." Her voice was muffled now against his shoulder. "Every new job I had, I would notice something off and worry that there'd be trouble so I'd quit rather than sit there saying nothing."

Logan drew out of the hug and sat next to his mom on the couch.

"What kinds of things were off?"

"Nothing major, nothing like at Hart & Preston. Usually just off-color jokes. It's ironic that at probably every other place, it would have actually helped for me to say something, but I couldn't risk it.

"Finally, at my last job, at the law office, I learned there are limits on when you can file these types of claims. Having a deadline made me realize I had to make a choice one way or another. I waited as long as I could. I hoped it would be all settled before you went to school. I didn't do it for the money, but if there's even a little, it would help you so much."

Logan shook his head.

"I don't need the money."

She gave him a sad smile.

"You do, sweetie, but it's nice of you to say that. I wanted to be able to send you off with at least something, but things have been taking so long. Apparently my lawyers are trying to reach out to other women who worked there to see if they can build a bigger case—"

Logan held up a hand.

"I don't need all the details, Mom," he said, not sure he could listen to much more without needing to hit something. He felt so totally powerless to help her. "I know enough."

"You know enough to see why you can't be with Cassie," said his mom. "You can't get mixed up with people like this, Logan. I know it's important for Columbia to make these kinds of connections, but these people, they're not like us."

"What's that supposed to mean?" Logan was surprised at how angry he sounded. He scolded himself. This was not the moment to attack his mom, not when she was already under so much stress. He lowered his voice. "She's not like that."

"Logan, I'm sure she's a sweet girl, but if this is how he treats his employees, how do you think he treats his family? People like that have so much money, they don't even care what they do to others. Your dad was the same, too."

A familiar rage filled him when he thought about his dad. His mom couldn't really think Cassie was like that asshole, could she? Just because her dad had been so horrible, didn't mean Cassie was.

"I said she's not like that!" Logan stood up, trying desperately to keep calm but his hands balled into fists at his sides.

"Why are you messing up the one good thing in my life right now?"

"I'm not trying to mess it up. I just…" His mom stopped and took a deep breath. "You wanted to know why you can't be with Cassie as anything more than a classmate. Now you know. It's just too complicated. I'm sorry."

"No, I'm sorry, Mom." Logan suddenly felt sick at how he'd reacted. He released his hands from fists and could see his mom relax a little, too. "Thank you for telling me."

"Cassie probably already knows, so it just makes sense for you to know, too." His mom looked up at him with sad eyes. "Maybe when this is all over, things can be different between the two of you."

Logan frowned. There was no way Cassie could know about this, or she wouldn't be spending all this time with him.

Would she?

His heart pounded in his ears as he gave his mom a hug and told her goodnight. He couldn't sort it all out now. He needed time to process.

It was past midnight and he'd been ready to fall right into bed but he was suddenly wide awake. He made his way to his bedroom in the office, knowing his mom preferred to crash on the couch when she was at the lake.

Hideki was waiting for him in the office but Logan shook his head the instant he saw his cousin's eager face.

"Not right now, man."

"Aw, come on! You gotta give me something!"

Logan wasn't sure what his face was doing, but one look and Hideki hung his head.

"Fine, whatever, keep it all to yourself."

As he left the room, Logan considered telling him everything, and getting his opinion on it. Cassie must know already. How could she not?

It was all just too convenient. She came to his house, trying to help him out. Had her dad sent her? Every little interaction he started to analyze, trying to remember if she'd ever mentioned his mom. He scrolled through their messages, realizing how little she really talked about herself, preferring to ask him questions. Was she getting more information on his family to relay back to her dad?

All his life he'd been lied to by so many people. He should have known better than to trust someone like her. His mom was right. When you had that much money, you couldn't really care about anyone else. He'd learned that early on and was reminded every birthday and Christmas that went by when it was just him and his mom.

And yet...

Cassie wouldn't have kissed him if she didn't like him... right? He hadn't expected to like her as much as he did. If he was being totally honest with himself, he'd been relieved for her offer of help and information. New York was exciting but a big unknown. Did it really matter why or how she'd started talking to him? She must like him. Girls didn't go around kissing guys just to resolve legal battles between their families, did they?

He groaned and sunk into his pillow. He could tell you the square root of pi, name all 400 species of sharks that existed, but he didn't know a thing about girls. Would Columbia be able to teach him that?

Deciding for the moment to hang on to the trust he instinctively felt for Cassie, he sent her a message. When she replied in less than a minute, his heart flooded with relief. She really liked him. He didn't know why, but in this moment, it was enough. All this would be sorted out tomorrow. For now, he needed sleep.

CHAPTER NINETEEN

CASSIE HAD NOT EXPECTED to find herself in front of
Logan's house quite so soon after the fireworks, especially not
this early in the morning. It was much too early to be anywhere,
let alone awake and attempting any kind of serious conversation,
but she'd spent a restless night trying to figure out what she
wanted.

She didn't want Spencer that was for sure. And she had
wanted Marissa to hook up with him, hadn't she? The anger and
hurt she'd felt when she'd seen them together had to have been
irritation, not jealousy. How could she be jealous when she
had Logan?

Logan. Even thinking his name sent shivers through her
body. She wanted him in that pure and perfect, all-consuming
way that starts to eat away at you in little bits and pieces. Even
when she was thinking of her former best friend, Logan hovered
at the edge of her mind, tempering her anger with a giddy light-
ness. In the space of just a few weeks, she'd gone from not
knowing his name to every time she pictured his face it felt like
a vice around her heart. Did he feel the same? The thought
filled her with both joy and dread.

She had to tell him what she'd done. He had to know. If this was going to be anything serious, if she was going to be different and not live the same life she'd had the past four years, and not live a life like her parents, she had to stop lying. Logan had never lied to her, not once; he didn't have a reason to. She couldn't let her feelings for him get too deep without him knowing everything.

So now here she was, in full makeup the night after the Fourth of July, a giant travel mug of tea next to her. She'd sent Logan a quick *I need to see you* as she'd quietly made her way out of the house less than fifteen minutes ago. Now she sent another, her fingers trembling.

I'm in front of your house.

Cassie vaguely noticed a blue car that hadn't been there the night before, but brushed it aside when she saw Logan step out the front door. Her heart fluttered at the memory of his lips on hers, and she gripped the steering wheel to keep from running out to him.

She seriously had to get herself under control.

Of course, she launched herself at him the second he got in the car. Her attack was met with an equally eager response from Logan. His hands were in her hair and cradling her head, their mouths crashing into each other with an intensity that was borderline inappropriate for seven o'clock in the morning.

He seemed to realize this at the same time as she did, and pulled out of the embrace, breathless.

"We shouldn't stay here." He glanced back at the house, his eyebrows drawn together.

She pulled away from the house without a word, and headed down to the lake. It would still be full of campers from the night before, but at least they could park without the chance of his family witnessing their making out.

He didn't say anything during the short trip, and if he hadn't just greeted her with such enthusiasm, Cassie would have been worried that something was wrong. But his face was serious, his eyes and mouth pulled down in such a thoughtful expression, that her heart started to beat faster for a completely different reason.

"Is everything okay?" she said, pulling into a spot into the day lot. Did he already know what she wanted to tell him?

"Did your parents notice you were gone last night?" Logan was looking at his hands.

"I don't think so, my sister covered for me," she said. Not the entire truth, but he didn't need to know how awful her family really was. Or that her parents still wanted to see her with Spencer. "But I caught Marissa and Spencer hooking up in my guest house last night when I got home." Cassie let the words spill out of her in a rush. Logan looked up at her, an eyebrow raised. "Yeah, I know. I don't really care but..." She shook her head. She'd sort through those feelings later. "Did you get grilled by your cousin when you got home?"

Logan bit his lip.

"No not Hideki...Hey, how's your dad?"

Well that was a weird question.

"Fine. Better since mom and Di are here. Why?"

He sighed and looked out the window, away from her. Her heart beat faster at the faraway look in his eyes. They'd barely been apart for 8 hours. What could have possibly happened during that time? She leaned against her door, dizzy with anxious anticipation.

"My mom was there when I got home last night," he said, still facing the window. "She said...She said I can't see you anymore."

Anger bubbled up inside of Cassie to replace the panic that had started to course through her veins. As if it wasn't bad enough her parents were deciding her life for her, now Logan's mom wanted in on the action?

"Why not?" She tried to keep her voice even. Cassie could think of a pretty big reason why not but her pride had been hurt. It was one thing to know she wasn't good enough for Logan, but to have someone else say it was a harsh reminder of how the world saw her.

Logan shifted in the seat, still looking out the window. Cassie wished he would look at her. Not being able to see his eyes or his reactions was maddening. What was going on inside his head?

"She said..." He turned to look at her, at last. His down-turned eyes and lips sent a chill through her. Pity was not something she was used to seeing aimed at her. "She said she's suing your dad. That he forced her to quit when she complained about how he was treating the women at work."

Cassie stared at him, open-mouthed, a cold wave of shock bursting in her chest. The vagueness of his answer sent her mind into overdrive. Her mouth was completely dry, and she had to swallow a few times to be able to squeak out her question.

"How...how was he treating them?"

Logan flushed.

"Did you really not know about this?"

She shook her head, trying to process the thought of her father doing ... something to the women at his office. And being so horrible as to fire someone for complaining? He wasn't like that. Maybe he was a little hard on his daughters sometimes, but he was their dad. He was supposed to be making sure they were prepared for life.

"Jokes and making them uncomfortable and...touching them," Logan said as he shifted in the seat again, looking like he'd rather be anywhere else. "No one said anything, except my mom. She thought maybe the men just didn't realize what they were doing, but when she talked to them, they told her to keep her mouth shut or she'd never get another job."

It was suddenly hard to breathe. Cassie fumbled to open the door, and leaned her head out, taking in big gulps of cool morning air. The salty tang of the lake bit her tongue. She replayed the words in her head. Uncomfortable...touching...bile rose in her throat and she choked it back.

She heard the passenger door click open and Logan's quick step as he made his way around the car to her.

"I'm so sorry," he said, pulling her out of the car and upright into his arms. "I thought you knew. My mom said you probably did."

Tears had sprung up in her eyes and she tried to blink them away, grateful he couldn't see her as she buried her face in his chest. He smelled just the same as he had the night before, all ginger and citrus.

"So your mom doesn't want you to be with me because of the lawsuit?" Her voice was muffled but she was afraid to look up at him, to see even more pity in his eyes she did not deserve. "Or because my dad is an asshole and she thinks I am too?"

"I guess...I mean, I don't know. She said other stuff about your family."

That didn't surprise her. She thought of the nice cozy house Logan's aunt and uncle had and what a normal family they were. No pressure to be some perfect family with a perfect daughter hosting perfect parties. No lying about what they did, all the time. Logan could just be himself. And with him she'd started to feel like herself, too. A better version of herself. But now that was all slipping away.

The tears finally started to fall in between gasping breaths.

"I'm j-just like h-him," she sobbed.

"No, you're not," He pulled her tight and kissed the top of

her head. "I don't care what my mom says. I know you're different. You're different than all of them."

Her heart swelled at this. He had no idea how big a compliment that was.

And that it was completely untrue.

CHAPTER TWENTY

LOGAN COULDN'T STAND LIARS. His dad was one. Had his mom lied about Cassie knowing?

No, she'd just said Cassie *probably* knew. And Cassie hadn't lied about her dad—she honestly hadn't known. He'd felt relief and guilt at the same time. She wasn't with him because of some secret plan of her dad. But Logan hated that he'd made her cry. It wasn't how he'd wanted the morning to go.

He was leaning against the car with Cassie buried in his arms as she cried, looking out over the lake. It was so peaceful here. What if they'd gone off to school without knowing? Would it have been worse to deal with this from a distance? Or better? Either way, the choice had been made and they knew now and would just have to work through it. Together.

Slowly, Cassie's sobs calmed and she started sniffing.

"Hey, it'll be okay," Logan said softly as he squeezed her tight. Her soft body molded to him perfectly. Her hair was a mess, her eyes ringed in red, but she'd never looked more beautiful. His chest tightened. "I'm not going to stay away from you just because my mom tells me to."

After all, his mom hadn't outright asked him to break up with

Cassie. She'd just made it clear that was what she wanted. But he'd made up his mind the second he'd seen Cassie's reaction to the news. It wasn't fair to punish her for something her father had done.

"You're not going to listen to your mom?" Cassie's eyes were wide and disbelieving.

Logan shrugged.

"Do you always do what your parents want?"

She didn't say anything, so he had his answer.

"It's not like I'll parade you around or anything." He flushed. "Not that I would do that anyway! I mean, I want to. I mean, I'm not—"

She put a hand to his mouth to stop him and giggled a little. The sound flooded him with warmth.

"Let's just forget it. It's their issue, not ours. We'll be in New York in, like, eight weeks. Far away from this."

"Maybe I don't want to leave anymore," Logan said, suddenly realizing what going away to school would mean. "I don't want to leave my mom dealing with all of this on her own."

Cassie looked at him with wide and angry eyes.

"Logan, don't be ridiculous. You can't give up a full ride to Columbia. This is your shot."

"My shot at what? Another four years of high school working my ass off while the rich kids party?"

Cassie jerked back, and Logan felt like an idiot.

"That's not what I meant—"

"No, it's fine, you're right." Cassie sniffed and stepped back, out of his arms. "New York will be really different than it is here. It's normal to be nervous about it."

"That's why they did the match thing though, right?" Logan said. "Do you think that's why your dad asked you to do it instead? Because of the thing with my mom?"

She looked down at the ground, kicking at a loose stone.

The sun had started to make its way up in the sky, and she was bathed in the early morning light, her hair shimmering.

"I don't know," she said softly. She looked up at him and shook her head, her eyes red. "I don't want to talk about him anymore."

Neither did Logan.

"Do you want to go get breakfast?" Logan swallowed hard. He shouldn't be nervous asking her out on a date after all that had happened in the past 12 hours. But he still was.

"I'd like that," she said, and gave him her little half-smile. His breath caught in his throat.

"I don't need to be at the restaurant until later tonight," he said. He'd planned on just spending the day with Hideki playing video games, but there were suddenly much more interesting possibilities. "So we could spend the day doing...whatever you want. Not talking about any of this."

"I'd like that," she said again, and placed her hand gently in his. Her other hand slid up to his shoulder. "How are you feeling? It must be sore after last night. We should take it easy today."

He let out a chuckle.

"It's fine. Don't get all bossy Cassie on me."

She raised an eyebrow. He cleared his throat.

"So, where to for breakfast?"

THROUGH THE BRILLIANT storytelling of his cousin, Logan's mother thought he'd been out with Hideki all day. A few texts over breakfast had gotten the details straight so that by the time he walked in the house to change for his shift at the restaurant, his mom was already on her way back to Helena.

He'd told her all about his morning run and a day at the lake with Hideki when she'd called before leaving.

He felt guilty lying to her, but he'd never promised his mom he'd stay away from Cassie. She'd just said he *couldn't* be with her. Logan had already decided he wanted to be. What difference did it make if it was now or in two months once they were New York?

Cassie and Logan had talked all day about what they'd do once they were there. All the places she wanted to show him, all the things they'd do together. Central Park in the fall and Rockefeller Center at Christmas and Times Square on New Year's Eve...

He knew it was a long shot that once they were there she'd even still want him. They'd gone from strangers to inseparable in less than a month. And yet, he couldn't help but picture it along with her. New York would give them freedom from their parents and from the worry this sudden legal drama was bringing them both.

But then he also thought of his mom, alone and dealing with everything. He told himself after his call with her that it would be the last time he lied to her. She'd been honest with him, so he had to do the same.

Exhausted from the day and his long shift at the restaurant, Logan was not in the mood for Hideki's teasing on the ride home, but he knew it was his payment for all his cousin had done for him that day.

"Time to spill, lover boy," Hideki snickered as Logan got into his truck.

Logan groaned and covered his face.

"I can't have, like, one private thing in my life?"

"Of course not. Especially not when I had to lie to your mom about it."

"You've lied to her plenty of times about stupid stuff we did."

"Yeah, but she looked super upset today."

Logan's stomach flipped. Definitely no more lying to his mom. He hated feeling this way.

"Do you know what's up?" Hideki asked him.

Logan shook his head without any guilt this time. His mom hadn't asked him to keep the lawsuit a secret, but he knew she wouldn't want her sister and family to know. Not until it was all over one way or another. They'd just want to step in and help and they already did more than enough.

"What did you guys get up to today?" Hideki waggled his eyebrows. "Checking a few things off the BSE list?"

Logan rolled his eyes. The only entries about girls had been pretty vague: "do stuff with girls" and "do more stuff with girls."

"Just hanging out by the lake," he said. "Use your imagination."

"Hanging out by the lake...talking?" Hideki raised an eyebrow.

"Sure," Logan said with a smile. "Talking about the best summer ever."

Hideki rolled his eyes and left it at that, satisfied for the moment to make up whatever he wanted about the day Logan had spent with Cassie.

Meanwhile, Logan leaned back in the seat and closed his eyes, reliving every second of it in the privacy of his own mind.

CHAPTER TWENTY-ONE

———————————————

"DI, DID YOU KNOW?"

Cassie burst into her sister's room, not bothering to knock. Di put down her book and sighed.

"I assume you mean about Mom and Dad?"

"Yes! No wait, what?" Cassie stopped short, thrown off of her laser focus on finding out the truth about this lawsuit. Di was in law school; he might have talked to her about it.

Di looked at her, frowning.

"What are you talking about?" she asked Cassie.

"No, what are *you* talking about? Are Mom and Dad getting a divorce?"

Di sighed again.

"I don't know. But after what's been happening, they're seeing a marriage counselor."

"What exactly has been happening?" Cassie's voice was on edge now. She'd been thinking about it ever since she left Logan on his front porch, a lingering kiss cut short by the ever-present Hideki. She could have spent all night with Logan, and wanted to wait for him outside the restaurant until he finished his shift. Maybe she should have, instead of hearing whatever Di was about to tell her. Cassie's heart was pounding in her chest so loudly, she was afraid she wouldn't be able to actually hear what her sister was about to say.

"There's a situation," said Di, her brow furrowed and mouth turned down. "With a former employee."

Cassie bit her lip. She wanted to ask about what Logan had told her, but held off. Hearing this side of things could be helpful.

"A former employee? One of the contractors?"

Di shook her head.

"A woman. It's raising a lot of issues between Mom and Dad."

Cassie wasn't surprised. If what Logan had told her was true—and she had no reason to think he was lying—then it couldn't have been easy for her picture-perfect mom to accept.

"Is that why she wasn't here at the beginning of the summer?"

Di nodded. Cassie sank down into the bed next to her. The room was pretty bare, since Di was almost never at the lake, but there were still touches of her big sister sprinkled around: a teddy bear from when they were kids, a framed picture of the four of them.

"Honestly, I'm surprised they lasted this long," said Di, putting her arm around Cassie's shoulder. "But they're both so involved in everything in Helena, they can't risk something like this."

"Risk? He's not the mayor or anything." She leaned into her big sister, breathing in her familiar perfume. The same one as their mom. Cassie had gotten her own bottle of it on graduation day, but hadn't taken it out of the box yet. It still seemed too much of a grown up thing to do, and this was her last summer as a kid. Sort of.

"Yeah, but Dad's business depends a lot on people liking

him, and his family. They've been bugging me a lot about moving back. The internship this summer in Helena got them way too excited."

Cassie wrinkled her nose.

"Why would you do that? California is awesome!"

Di laughed.

"Still time to change your mind. Stanford would be right down the road from me."

Cassie sighed and pulled away. This wasn't the time to rehash her decision about college and she hadn't even gotten the answers she wanted. But she wasn't going to get them from her sister, apparently.

"I'll think about it," she said with a smile. With a final hug from her sister, Cassie went in search of the one person who would have the answers—her dad.

CASSIE WALKED AROUND THE HOUSE, her dad nowhere to be found and his fishing pole missing from the hall closet. Going out on the lake in the early evening was not really the best time to catch anything, but maybe he needed the quiet after the party last night. She wandered into her parents' room, looking for her mom instead and was surprised to find her packing a bag.

"I thought you were staying all week," Cassie said, sitting on the bed like she used to when she was little.

"There are some things I need to take care of in Helena."

Cassie looked at her closely, trying to see the emotion behind her eyes. Everything she'd learned about dealing with people had been from her mom. Every movement was calculated to make others feel a certain way. It had been helpful in high school when Cassie needed to get the other cheerleaders to agree, or to convince a teacher to extend a deadline for her.

But now it just felt fake. She was surrounded by lies. Her parents had both been lying to her all summer. Diana had only told her the half of it. Logan was the only one who cared about her feelings and had been willing to share everything he knew.

And Cassie still shouldn't be totally honest with him. Because that's not how they did it in her family.

"What kind of things?" Cassie swung her feet against the side of the bed and let them fall against the solid oak bed frame.

Thunk, thunk. Thunk, thunk.

"Just business things," her mom said, folding a red cardigan in careful thirds before placing it on top of an identically folded blue one in her open suitcase.

"Your business or Dad's business?"

Her mom glanced up with a look that might have even been panic, before smoothing her face into a smile.

"It's nothing for you to worry about. Just focus on Columbia. I'm so happy you finally decided. I told everyone at the party."

Despite everything, Cassie's chest swelled at the pride in her mom's voice.

"I started talking to someone who might know about an apartment you could rent, but when I turned around, you'd disappeared."

And just as quickly, the pride was replaced with a sinking dread as her mom shot her a pointed glare.

"Sorry about that," Cassie said. "I just couldn't handle seeing Spencer there with Marissa."

Her mom closed her eyes and took a deep breath.

"These things happen, sweetheart," she said, opening her eyes. She went to her nightstand and picked up a few trinkets to add to her bag. "You have to learn to just put on a brave face and deal with people who have disappointed you."

"You mean lie?" Cassie kept her voice even, just as she'd been taught.

Her mother clicked her tongue in annoyance.

"It's not lying to learn to live civilly with others," she said, with a glance at Cassie's feet hanging over the edge of the bed. "You can't go around yelling and crying whenever you feel like it."

"I know," Cassie mumbled, her feet banging again. *Thunk, thunk.* "That's why I left. So I didn't cry."

Her mom stopped her packing and pursued her lips.

"I know we expect a lot of you, Cassie. But it's only because we know you're capable of it. We've set everything up so that you and your sister can have the best life possible. I don't think it's asking too much when there are certain expectations for your behavior that go along with that life."

Thunk, thunk, went her feet against the bed.

"Cassie," her mom shot her a warning glance at her feet. She stopped, her foot held high, ready to fall again.

She knew what her mom expected of her. What everyone expected of her.

But what about her expectations of them? Everyone had been lying to her all summer, and now she was in an awful position. She believed Logan, but what was she supposed to do about it? Yell at her parents? Demand her dad pay his mom?

Cassie sighed and lowered her foot slowly, and silently. Her mom smiled and nodded then turned her attention back to packing her bag.

Cassie waited to see if there was anything else, but knew that was all she would be getting out of her mom. At least until her next visit, whenever that would be.

CHAPTER TWENTY-TWO

AS THE HOT July days slowly slid into August, Logan was with Cassie every second he wasn't working. In her car, at the lake, in the restaurant parking lot after work. It was like he was trying to make up for years of no kissing in a matter of weeks.

He didn't know what she told her parents. Maybe they didn't even notice when she wasn't home. He'd avoided his aunt's questions more than a few times, telling her he was hanging out with friends. It wasn't technically a lie, but she'd still purse her lips and narrow her eyes. If she asked him outright if he was with Cassie, he told himself he wouldn't lie. But his aunt never asked. So...

They sent messages back and forth like breathing.

So this hammerhead thing you have, she sent one day when he was cleaning houses. It was a constant stream of connection. The longest they ever went without messaging when they weren't together or sleeping was probably five minutes tops. Hideki had tried to institute a no phone rule during their video game sessions, but it hadn't lasted more than a night.

What about it? Logan was still embarrassed he'd told her about it. It was one thing to like a random artist, but sharks weren't cool. Were they?

Have you ever seen one in real life? she asked

I haven't even seen a fish other than what's in the lake, he admitted.

What?? How is that possible??

Now he was really embarrassed.

No aquariums in Helena. He sent a shrugging emoji along with it; it wasn't his fault their town was too small for anything bigger than a petting zoo.

A few minutes went by before she sent another message.

Where can you even see hammerheads in the wild?

Costa Rica, came his immediate reply.

He didn't even have to look it up. While his mind and money were all focused on New York, when he'd started pulling in bigger tips from bartending, he'd let himself dream a little bit about what else he might be able to do. There were so many places he'd like to see, and sharks in Costa Rica were top of the list. He'd never have enough; school would eat into all of it he was sure, but that's where his mind would drift off to as he scrubbed toilets. A beach somewhere where the water was actually warm.

If we go, will you tell me all about hammerheads and their mating dance?

Now when he daydreamed of sandy beaches, Cassie was right there beside him.

ONE NIGHT they were in her bedroom, curled up on the bed. It was raining hard outside, or they'd have been at their usual spot at the lake. It was extremely cozy and comfortable, but Logan couldn't relax.

They were so close, every single part of their bodies that were touching sent little shivers of electricity through him. The fruity smell of her shampoo was invading his senses, making it impossible to concentrate on anything. He didn't even know what movie they were watching. Something action, not romantic, so she wouldn't think he had any grand plans for her. He was still getting used to the idea that he was allowed to kiss her anytime he wanted.

Well, not anytime. The only reason they were at her house tonight was because Cassie's parents and sister were out and she'd pretended to be sick to stay home. He knew it was rare for her parents and sister to all be together at the lake house, so he was surprised and thrilled that she'd wanted to spend the time with him instead. Still...

"I don't like sneaking around," he said. His gut was shouting at him, telling him to just shut up and enjoy what he had. The past month had more than he could ever have hoped for. BSE did not even begin to describe it.

"It'll be fine once we're in New York." She snuggled against him, and his chest tightened. She sounded so sure of herself when she talked about the future. It was easy for her, knowing what to expect. As excited as he was, the thought of leaving everything he knew still freaked him out more than he wanted to admit.

But having Cassie there would make it feel more like home. He reached down to place a kiss on her head, and she turned her face up to him. A deeper kiss started, his arms curving around her back, the feel of her skin hot beneath his hands. The tiny tank top she was wearing suddenly took up an enormous amount of his attention, and he tried to make sure his hands only ventured where there was fabric. He didn't dare attempt anything else but she shifted beneath him and when he ran his hand down her arm she let out a soft sigh that made his heart beat ten times faster.

Maybe tonight he would slide his hand a little higher. Maybe tonight they would—

"Cassie! Where are you?"

They broke apart, their ragged breaths hot on each other's face as her wide eyes stared into Logan's.

"Hide!" she hissed, and he rolled off the bed in a move worthy of the spy film they were watching. He scooted underneath the bed, her panicked face peering down at him. Even over the beating of his heart he noticed her lips were still red from kissing.

So beautiful.

She smiled and he flushed; he hadn't meant to say it out loud.

Safely under the bed, hidden from her family and his own embarrassment, Cassie arranged the covers so they hung over the side. It was dark, but he was safe.

"What are you watching?" A girl's muffled voice reached Logan's ears.

"Nothing, Di. What's up? I thought you were all out to eat."

She sounded so calm, so natural. Hideki needed to learn her secrets.

"Well we're back. Mom and Dad want to talk to you."

"About what?"

"I'll let them explain."

Logan worried the intense pounding of his heart would give him away. There was no way they couldn't hear it.

"Is he finally going to explain this whole sexual harassment thing?"

Di sighed.

"That's not really what it is."

Cassie snorted.

"It's a wrongful termination suit and he's taking care of it. That's what he wants to talk to you about. You might need to give testimony."

"What? Why?" Her calm veneer cracked and she sounded panicked.

"You were on work sites with him this summer. You can tell them he treats his employees with respect."

The ice cold silence seeped under the bed and trickled down Logan's spine.

"But just because Dad didn't do anything while I was there doesn't mean—"

"You really think he's like that? That he's horrible to his employees?" Her sister raised her voice to an angry yell that had Logan sweating and cowering in his hiding spot. Cassie had mentioned she was in law school but he hadn't pictured someone quite so intimidating. And he couldn't even see her!

"I don't know," Cassie answered, her voice low.

Di clicked her tongue and sighed again.

"He's your dad, Cass. After everything he's done for you, you have to help him."

There was a pause, and the bed sank down above Logan's head as Cassie sat down.

"Speaking of helping...How did the Huntingtons help him?"

"What do you mean?"

"The night Spencer and I broke up, he said we should be grateful to his family...when I asked Dad what it meant he said it was just business contacts."

What was that about? She'd never mentioned that to Logan, but they didn't really talk about Spencer. Logan held his breath, not wanting to miss a single word.

"Why?"

"If I'm going to lie for him, I want to know everything."

"It's not lying, Cass. Did you see him do anything inappropriate this summer? Or ever?"

There was a pause. She must have shaken her head.

"See? You know this whole suit is a bunch of crap. I see it all the time in case studies for school. People trying to game the system, make the most they can from employers."

Spoken like someone who'd never had to work a day in her life. She could leave law school tomorrow and live well the rest of her life. Logan bit down on his tongue to keep an annoyed growl from escaping his lips.

"What did the Huntingtons do?" Cassie's voice was stronger now.

"They just introduced him to some lawyers. Good ones. And kept a lot of stuff out of the papers. His business was suffering a lot earlier this year."

"Because of the suit?"

Another pause.

"And other things. With Mom and everything."

"She's here tonight."

"She made up her mind to stick with him."

Cassie sucked in a breath. She'd never mentioned any of this to Logan. He let out a shaky breath, as quietly as possible. All they'd done for weeks was make out and dream about New York. Her mom, the Huntingtons...what else had she avoided talking about with him?

"So? Will you help him?" Diana pressed her.

There was another pause. Logan shifted underneath the bed, his heart racing.

"I'll think about it," was all Cassie said.

CHAPTER TWENTY-THREE

WHEN CASSIE LEANED over to help Logan out from under the bed, she wasn't sure who looked more upset.

They'd avoided talking about her dad ever since that morning after the Fourth of July. It was easier to focus on New York and dreaming of a new life far away from all of this. They both wanted to escape, for different reasons. Logan wanted a new life, and he deserved one; he'd worked so hard to get where he was. Cassie wanted to leave behind the mess of a family she was a part of.

But she knew she could never escape, not really. Di was right. If her dad wanted her to do something, she would do it. The entire reason she was with Logan now was because her dad had asked her to be nice to him. Guilt washed away the pure bliss that had been shooting through her just ten minutes ago. This wasn't the way she'd wanted Logan to hear about her parents' problems. Would he guess that she was hiding other things?

Now at least it made sense why her dad had known who Logan was. And why he didn't want Logan to suspect his bike accident had anything to do with her. Her family didn't want another legal battle with his. She thought back to her mom's comment on how expensive an apartment in New York would be. While Di had made it sound like their parents were working things out, a divorce would be expensive, if it ever came to that. Could they not *afford* another legal battle? The thought of not having enough money for something was completely foreign to Cassie.

Even if they could afford it, what would happen if Cassie refused to testify? How could she face her dad, her family, knowing that she'd stood against them? Would Columbia even be an option for her? Would any college?

There was no rebelling possible, no way out. She had to support her dad, or he wouldn't support her. It was what everyone expected her to do.

"What are you going to do?" Logan said as he took her offered hand and stood up.

"I don't know yet." Her voice trembled.

Logan took a step back and dropped her hand.

"You're going to help your dad."

"I said I don't know yet!" Her eyes flashed. "This is hard for me. I don't know what to think."

"It's not really that complicated." He crossed his arms over his chest, eyes narrowed. "He's not a good guy. You're an adult, you don't have to do what he wants."

"But he's my dad, you know?" Tears glittered at the edges of her eyes. All month he'd never said a word about her dad, and while she knew he probably hated him for what he'd done to his mom, he couldn't expect her to feel the same way, could he?

"Actually, I don't know." Logan set his jaw. "Mine left when I was four."

Cassie's eyes widened and raised a hand to her open mouth.

"Logan, I had no idea—"

"It's fine," he said quickly, waving a hand. "We don't have to talk about it. He's not a part of my life."

"Not at all?" Cassie sat down on the bed and looked up at him. Logan started to pace.

"No," he said firmly, his arms swinging beside him as he walked back and forth. Had they been talking about anything else, she might have teased him about how much like a shark he looked right now, with his angry gaze and puffed out chest. "He made so many promises..."

Cassie held her breath, not sure she wanted to hear more. Logan had already been through so much. How much more pain could one person have in their life?

"Every year it would be the same. Birthdays, holidays, all he would send were cards with promises of phone calls and visits. He never called. He never came."

His eyes shone with tears that she knew he'd never let fall.

"He sent stuff all the time when I was little." He made a weird harsh laughing sound. "He was totally loaded. My mom told me later he never sent any child support though. And she didn't have the money to go after him for it. She told herself the presents to me were enough. But all I wanted was to see him.

"When I was twelve I finally got him on the phone and told him to stop sending me stuff. I didn't want anything else from him if he couldn't keep his promises and visit."

Cassie's heart was breaking for the stubborn little boy that had grown into such a strong young man who never wanted anyone's help.

"And that was the last I heard from him. No more presents, no more calls, nothing."

"Oh, Logan." Cassie made to stand up, but he put out a hand.

"Don't, okay? I know what I went through is totally different than this. And I may be a little biased and assume all dads are assholes."

"I don't know what mine is like with other people," she said. "I only know him as my dad. That's what makes this so hard."

Logan sighed and collapsed onto the bed next to her, covering his face with his hands.

"My whole life is hard," he mumbled into his hands. Cassie hesitated for a brief moment, but put a hand on his back. She felt him relax a little underneath her touch.

"It's nice to know we have something else in common now," she said, trying to lighten the mood. "Even if it's just complicated feelings about our dads."

He let out a chuckle.

"Of all the things for me to have in common with Cassie Hart, a rich jerk for a dad wasn't what I thought it would be."

Cassie let out a giggle. Laughing wouldn't change anything, but what else could they do?

With a sigh, Logan leaned back on the bed. Cassie followed suit and curled up against him. He had been through so much and had still turned out so smart and hardworking and...perfect. Her heart filled with the strongest desire to help him, in every possible way.

"I guess if everyone is back, I'll need to sneak back out?" he murmured into her hair. His arms were wrapped tightly around her. She snuggled even closer against his chest, needing to feel every part of him.

"Or you could just stay here until they all fall asleep," she said, turning her head to look up at him. He gazed down at her through half lowered lids and she bit her bottom lip. "Or you could hide in my bed all night and leave tomorrow morning."

He sucked in a breath and leaned over for a kiss. It started out so softly, his lips just barely brushing hers. Then he pressed himself against her and his arms gripped her even tighter. She opened her mouth, their tongues swirling together as she sighed into him. Her hands went to his hair, pulling him tightly to her.

Despite the past few weeks of doing this same thing, tonight she wanted more. Needed more. Everything was falling apart and he was the only thing that seemed steady in her life. And she knew she was inches away from losing him. As soon as he found out what she'd done to him, her father wouldn't be the only one he thought was a rich jerk.

Her whole family was such a mess. She couldn't wait to get away from them. Maybe once they were in New York she'd tell him. Once they were far away from everything else making their lives crazy.

She let out a soft moan as Logan's hand slid under her shirt, caressing her skin. Her entire body shivered against him. He pulled out of the kiss and looked into her eyes.

"Cassie I...want to tell you something." He took a deep breath. "I think I'm..."

He swallowed hard, his gaze intense. Her heart skipped a beat.

Could he really feel that way about her? With everything that was happening?

She didn't want him to say it, not out loud. Not until he knew everything. She leaned in and kissed him again, praying that she'd get a little more time with him before it all came crashing down.

"Cassie, where are you?"

For the second time that night, they pulled away from each other, breathless and panicked. It wasn't her sister outside the door this time.

It was her rich jerk of a dad.

CHAPTER TWENTY-FOUR

"CASSIE YOUR MOTHER and I need to talk to—"

Cassie's dad burst into the room without knocking. When he saw them both laying on the bed, Logan's hand halfway up Cassie's shirt, he stopped short, his eyes narrowing as his face turned bright red.

Logan shot up in bed, but Cassie was a bit slower to rise. She crossed her arms over her chest, while Logan stared wide-eyed at her dad seething in the doorway.

"I guess you're not feeling that sick anymore." His words were a simmering quiet volcano ready to burst.

"I was just leaving," Logan said, standing up.

"No, don't go," Cassie said, and grabbed his arm. She turned to her dad, her brows furrowed and her eyes flashing. "If you were Spencer he wouldn't care."

"If he were Spencer you wouldn't have lied to us," her dad said, crossing his own powerful arms over his chest. "I need to talk to you. Alone."

His eyes flicked to Logan, who swallowed hard. His palms were starting to sweat as he tried to keep his own rage under control. He'd gone back and forth tonight from having Cassie in his arms to her being ripped out of them, and back again. The ups and downs were starting to take a toll. He'd been about to tell her how he felt. He'd been thinking the words for days; they'd been on the tip of his tongue a hundred times. Was he actually a little relieved for the interruption? If he'd said it and she hadn't said it back, it would have been more than his poor tortured heart could handle for one night.

"Di already talked to me," said Cassie, still holding on to Logan's arm. He wanted to stay, to help her somehow. She wasn't used to standing up to her parents, and didn't seem to really know how. Not that Logan did either, but at least he knew what a good relationship looked like. An honest one. He'd seen her cry more than once over all this drama. He couldn't leave her now.

But her dad was starting to get really scary. A flare of protectiveness shot through Logan, and he sat back down next to her on the bed.

"Well, I need to talk to you again on the subject. Please leave, Logan."

Logan took a deep breath. *Please don't let it be my last,* he prayed.

"If Cassie wants me to stay, I'll stay." He looked right into his eyes. The volcano looked close to erupting and a rock settled in Logan's stomach. This was definitely not how he'd pictured the evening going. But he remembered what this man had done. What men like him did all the time. They hurt women like his mom and let girls like Cassie think that it was okay for guys to treat them like crap. Logan had seen how Spencer talked to her, and he'd probably learned it from his dad. Cassie just accepted that kind of behavior from hers.

"I won't say it again," her dad said, every word weighty with danger.

Their eyes met, both filled to the brim with barely controlled rage, but Logan burst first.

"Don't tell me what to do!" Logan cried. "You can't bully people just because you're rich! Money doesn't make you above the law." Cassie gasped next to him and dropped his hand.

Okay, maybe that had been too far.

"I can certainly ask someone to get out of my own house. Which I have multiple times now."

Logan stood his ground and set his jaw. He didn't know what her father's lowered eyes meant, but Cassie obviously did. She stood up and tugged on Logan's arm.

"Come on, I'll just take you home," she begged. His arm flexed beneath her hand. She tugged harder.

Logan took a deep breath and tried to still his beating heart. Yelling was one thing. But if he took a swing at her dad, not only would Columbia be out of the picture, so would any possible future he had, and everyone in the room knew it. Logan hated how much power her dad still had in this situation. It didn't matter if they were in his house, it would have been the same no matter where this had gone down.

But Cassie's dad looked at him with so much anger, it was impossible for Logan to not want to respond somehow. He had put up with so much crap at the restaurant and while cleaning houses over the years. People talking to him like he was nothing, like he didn't matter. He thought of the person who'd nearly ran him off the road, in their fancy red sports car, probably hadn't even noticed they'd nearly killed someone, so involved in their own perfect life. He thought of his dad, abandoning him just for wanting to spend time with him.

Cassie tugged a final time at his arm, and Logan shook his head, relaxing the fist his hand had made unconsciously. Her dad wasn't worth losing everything over. None of them were.

Throwing away his future wasn't going to change how they acted.

Thank goodness Cassie was different. She was there for him, worried about him. She cared about him. And if she asked him to stay, he'd stay. But right now, she was begging him to go.

"Come on!" she said, her hand on his back now.

With a final last glare at her dad, Logan let her push him out of the room.

CHAPTER TWENTY-FIVE

CASSIE DRAGGED Logan out of the house as fast as she could, hoping that by the time she got back, her dad would have cooled down.

And hopefully by then she'd know what to say to him. Logan had spilled his guts tonight to her, revealing so much more than she'd ever guessed about his father. She couldn't exactly betray that trust and tell her dad that 'sorry my new boyfriend was a jerk, but his own dad kind of sucks.'

Despite the current predicament, her heart leapt when she thought the word "boyfriend." They hadn't said anything official, but what else could he be? They were both leaving for New York in a few weeks, talking nonstop about what they'd do together once they were there, and had basically been attached at the lips for weeks on end. And Logan had been right on the verge of telling her how he felt. Her stomach clenched at the thought of three little words she'd never heard from any guy, ever. What would she have said in return? Cassie had never been this happy and excited with Spencer. She hoped Logan realized that.

At this precise moment, however, she was not particularly happy or excited. She was pretty freaking pissed off.

The rain had gotten harder as the night went on, and they were soaked before they even got to the car. She turned the heat on full blast, shivering a little as she started the engine. Logan trembled next to her, from cold or anger she wasn't sure.

"We didn't have to leave!"

Anger, then.

The rain was spattering against the windshield as the wipers struggled to keep up.

"Logan, you can't just say something like that to my dad." She tried to keep her voice calm. If there was a worse way for her parents to find out about Logan, she couldn't think of it. And then for him to mouth off like that to her dad... There was no coming back from that. The complete and total opposite of Spencer, her dad would hate Logan forever. She was already being made to choose between him and her family, and it had just gotten a million times harder.

"Of course I can! You know what he did to my mom!"

Cassie's face grew hot.

"What she says he did."

The silence that filled the car was deadly and thick. Cassie's heart fell into her stomach. She hadn't meant to say that. At least not in that way. She wanted to explain that she was still processing everything Diana had told her earlier, that she had to reconcile the image of her dad as loving father and horrible boss. Couldn't he see how hard it was to take a stand against her own family, and side with someone who she hadn't even met?

But as each second ticked by without any other sound but the pounding of rain against the car, it felt too late to take it back.

"Just let me out up here," Logan finally said, his voice an

empty monotone. He gestured to a side street but she drove right past it without even slowing down.

Cassie's eyes darted to his, but he was facing straight ahead, his arms folded against his chest.

"Don't be ridiculous, it's pouring," she said, trying to keep her voice light and free of any residual anger she may have. But there was no undoing the damage she'd done with just five little words.

"Just let me out."

"No."

"Let. Me. Out."

"Absolutely not."

"Cassie." From the corner of her eyes, she could see that he'd finally turned to face her. She dared another glance and his eyes were blazing, the hurt she'd caused him visible even in the darkness. "Stop the car right now."

She fixed her own glare right back at him.

"I said no."

Turning away from his angry face, she spotted a flash of neon green coming at her fast.

"Watch out!" Logan cried, as she swerved to avoid the biker.

With a gasp and a curse, she pulled the steering wheel over with a jerk, bumping along the edge of the road in a horribly familiar way. She cursed as branches swiped at the side of the car.

This can't be happening again.

With a few more bumps, she finally pulled to a stop. She leaned her face against the steering wheel, tears already starting to fall. A sob escaped her, and Logan's arm circled her shoulders.

"Hey, it's okay, the guy is fine." His voice was low and soothing, his anger gone in the face of her distress. "He gave us the finger as he rode away."

She curled into him awkwardly across the seats, but the weight of his arms caressing her back was a comfort. Already feeling queasy from the rollercoaster of emotions tonight, the last bit of fight left her in an instant.

"I just can't believe I did it again," she whispered, almost to herself.

His arms stilled against her back.

"What?" his voice was soft. Cassie gasped and sat up, taking in his wide eyes and open mouth.

"I mean..." She trailed off and took a deep breath.

This was it. She couldn't lie, not now. It wasn't how she'd planned on telling him, but had she ever really intended to? There had been countless times over the past few weeks she could have said something and she never had. She didn't have to think too hard about why. She was terrified that she would lose him. The one thing that was making her happy, the one person who made her feel like she could be something more than what everyone thought she was. The one person who didn't expect her to be anything but herself.

And now that one person was looking at her as a thousand emotions flashed across his face. Confusion, comprehension and finally...complete and total anguish. She held her breath, waiting for the final hammer to fall.

"My accident...that was you?" Her heart was breaking at his eyes so full of hurt. Hurt that she'd caused.

Tears traced jagged lines down her cheeks and her lips were trembling so much she could barely speak. All she could do was nod.

Pain and astonishment rippled across his face.

Another few beats of agonizing silence passed as he took this in. Her heart was beating harder than the rain hammering on the roof of the car.

"Is that why you were so crazy about getting me to the doctor?"

Hope gushed through her like a waterfall. Was he giving her a chance to explain?

"I wanted to be sure you were okay!" she cried, reaching out to him and taking his hand. "I was driving Spencer and Marissa home that night, I hadn't even been drinking. And then suddenly you were there and I swerved and—"

He pulled back and she withdrew her hand. The waterfall of hope dried up in an instant, leaving her empty inside, cracking around the edges.

"So you decided to pay me off, to make sure I didn't think it was you?" His face was twisted in rage.

He had jumped so quickly to the idea, it seemed ridiculous she'd ever been able to pull off the lie in the first place.

"My dad—"

"I don't want to hear about that asshole right now!"

Anger flared inside of her, despite everything. She didn't know how she felt about her dad right now but she didn't like to hear anyone else insulting him.

"He told me to do it," she tumbled over her words as they burst out as quickly as possible. He needed to hear everything in order to understand. "I dropped off Marissa and came back to check on you. I wanted to help, but you were so upset. When I went back home, my dad was there, and I told him what had happened. He was worried you'd ask for money if you knew it was me. He told me to spend time with you, so that you'd think I was nice and not suspect me."

"And the Columbia match program? Was that even real?" His eyebrows were drawn together as he slowly realized just how devious and horrible she was.

She shook her head.

"I thought up the Columbia thing, that wasn't him." She

could have said that was her dad's idea, too, but there had been enough lies between them. And it wasn't like he could hate her dad any more than he already did. "I saw your name in the new student group online and so I knew we had at least one thing in common."

Logan let out a choked laugh as he raked his hands through his hair.

"So there was no match. You just tricked me into fall—into liking you?"

Her heart twisted. He had been so close to telling her less than an hour ago how he felt. She should have known better than to think it could have been possible. He was so good, and so smart, and his family was so normal. Nothing fake or manipulative about any of them. She was stupid to think someone like her could ever have something so real with someone like Logan.

But what she felt for him was most definitely real, and the thought of losing him burned a wide hole inside of her.

"It wasn't a trick, Logan! I like you. I really like you." She reached out for him again, but he drew back against the car door. The rain lashed against the window. "I hadn't even officially chosen Columbia, and now, it's all I can think about. Going to New York with you and—"

He shook his head, and she stopped talking, her mouth going dry. Fissures started to appear around the edges of her heart.

"How can you expect me to believe that? I don't know what to believe." His eyes hardened and narrowed. "You seem to believe your dad, though, and do whatever he says."

"I don't want to, I want to change." The tears had started to fall again and she wiped them away, trying to keep her vision of him clear. She knew this would be the last time she'd see him and wanted to remember every angle of his gorgeous face, even twisted in anger the way it was now. "I felt like I was changing, with you. I could be someone different and New York would be so different and—"

He held up a hand, stopping her again.

"Don't. Just don't, Cassie."

His empty voice filled her with dread.

"Why should I believe anything some rich asshole has to say?"

And with that, he pushed open the door and stepped out into the rain.

CHAPTER TWENTY-SIX

WALKING home in the rain was a horrible, long, wet idea.

But Logan was so relieved to be away from Cassie that he didn't even notice the weather. He felt his phone buzz in his pocket a half dozen times, but didn't bother to take it out to see who it was. There was no way he was ruining his phone in the rain just so Cassie could give him some half-assed excuse for her lies.

He'd heard them all too many times from his dad.

Of course, tonight would be the night he finally told someone about that pain. He'd never even talked to Hideki about it. About growing up knowing that the man who was supposed to love you and be there for you was full of crap. Logan had learned how to see through the lies of others his entire life. All the fake happy smiles of people at school and at the restaurant were so clearly hiding something; he'd assumed everyone in that world of privilege was like that.

He thought he'd finally found someone who was real, despite the fake life she lived. It had taken a while to break down her joking and bossy defenses, but behind it she was glorious. She was funny and sweet and sexy and actually liked him, Logan Hanes, the poor kid without a father.

But all of that was a lie. He balled his fists into his jacket pockets, hunching against the biting rain. He should have known better. This is what he got for being stupid enough to trust someone like her. Walking home alone in the rain with his shoulder twinging because of an injury she'd fussed over while conveniently omitting the fact that she'd actually caused it nearly two months ago.

He would have felt sick if the burning rage would settle down.

Instead, he leaned into the rage, letting it warm him through the last mile of the dark and wet walk.

When he finally got home, it was much later than he realized. His aunt and uncle were waiting for him in the kitchen, their faces lined with worry.

"Logan!" cried his Aunt Caroline, shooting out of her chair when she heard the squelch of his shoes in the entryway. "What happened?"

"I don't want to talk about it," he mumbled, unzipping his soaking jacket. He let it drop at his feet, but picked it up when he heard his aunt's annoyed huff.

"I'll get you a towel," she said as she turned back toward the half bath right off the entryway. "Then you better call your mom."

Logan's burning rage was doused in an instant. Caroline grabbed the wet jacket out of his hand. He reached for the offered towel and rubbed it through his hair.

"Into the bathroom, everything off," she said. "Now." Her concerned tone from earlier had been replaced with an annoyance that was eerily like his mom's.

Logan obeyed silently, stripping to his boxers and wrapping

the towel around his waist. He handed off his clothes to his aunt, who was now giving him the stink eye.

Like this night could possibly get any worse.

"Call your mom," she repeated sternly as she rummaged in his wet clothes to pull out his phone. He took it with a small smile, his eyebrows raised.

"I'm really sorry for not calling. I didn't mean to make you worry."

"Hmm," was all she said as she looked him up and down, her eyebrows drawn together. As she made her way to the laundry room off the kitchen she called over her shoulder, "I'll make you some hot chocolate so you don't catch pneumonia."

His heart lifted a little. She couldn't be that mad at him if she was offering hot beverages.

At least Hideki was out and he'd only have his mom's questions to deal with. He made his way to the office and put on dry clothes before sitting down on the futon with his phone in hand.

Fifteen missed calls. He sighed and scrolled through them but his heart dropped when he realized they were all from his mom. Worry about what was happening overrode the aching pang that Cassie hadn't even tried to call him.

His mom answered on the first ring.

"What the hell, Logan!" She sounded furious. Worse than that time Hideki had convinced him to ride their bikes off a ramp into the lake when they were thirteen.

"I'm sorry?" he tried. What could she possibly have to be this mad about? Walking home in the rain hardly seemed to warrant this kind of anger.

"Cassie Hart? Really?"

A rock had suddenly taken the place of his stomach.

"Look it's not—"

"I called Caroline when you didn't pick up tonight." He

cringed as the heat in her voice singed even from through the phone. He had never heard her this angry. "She said you've been sneaking off for weeks. Weeks! Logan, I know you're an adult now, and can make your own choices but I thought with everything going on you'd understand why it just isn't possible for you two to—"

"It's over, Mom!" he cried, his words catching in his throat. He wasn't going to cry, not about Cassie and not in front of his mom. "She's not who I thought she was. So don't waste your breath. I should have listened to you."

There was a weighty silence on the other end. He could hear her breathing, slightly out of breath. She'd been preparing for a fight, and now, faced with his anger and hurt, he knew she'd want to protect him. Soothe him.

"Are you okay, sweetie?" Her voice was quiet, and it pained him all that much more to hear the concern in it.

"Not really," he said, deciding honesty was the best policy in this case. What good would it do to deny it? He was so pissed off and hurt, he wanted someone to take on a little of that with him. And his mom already hated the Harts.

"What happened?"

Logan hesitated. This was harder. Should he tell her about the accident? Would it change anything in terms of the lawsuit his mom was dealing with? He hadn't been hit, and as angry as he was at Cassie for lying, he did think she was telling the truth about being sober that night. There was nothing for his mom to gain in her case by adding on more deceitful behavior from the Harts.

"She's just...siding with her dad on the lawsuit," he said finally. It was still technically the truth, he decided. Just not all of it.

"Oh, Logan, I wish I could say that I'm surprised."

His anger flared at the insult, before he remembered he hated Cassie right now. He hated everything about her.

Though that also wasn't all of the truth.

"I am sorry that you're hurting," his mom said. She did sound sorry. And tired. Guilt shot through Logan again at knowing his mom had lost sleep yet again over him. "Do you want to come home early?"

"No, I still have three more weeks at the restaurant. I've been making crazy good tips at the bar."

There was silence again, and he wanted to say more. But how to explain what had happened? The hurt and anger were so raw; he just needed to be alone with the feelings for a while.

Besides, he had to start getting used to being alone without his mom there to help him.

"Okay, just let me know," she said softly. "Good night, sweetie."

"Night, Mom."

He tossed the phone down and fell back into the futon. His heart felt raw, his body ached everywhere, and there was so much swirling around in his head that he didn't think he'd be able to sleep for hours.

He turned over, settled in for a sleepless night, and passed out immediately.

CHAPTER TWENTY-SEVEN

CASSIE WASN'T sure what felt worse—losing Logan or finally agreeing to help her dad.

Her parents had at least waited until the next day to come talk to her. They must have been scared off by the wails coming from her room the night after dropping off Logan (*in a freaking thunderstorm,* her crushed heart reminded her daily). But the next morning they'd been waiting for her at the breakfast table, a united front ignoring every other pain than the one directly affecting them.

Did she realize the best way forward for everyone was for the family to stick together?

Yes, she saw that now.

Did she understand what they expect from her from here on out, if she still wanted to go to Columbia?

Yes, she understood.

But it still felt wrong. She had her parents back by her side but had lost something so much bigger. Her escape from this life and from who she didn't want to be was gone forever. She was still going to New York, but she'd be alone. Until she ran into whoever her parents had decided she needed to end up with, that is.

In the end, she decided it was just easier to not fight it and learn to deal with the unsettled feeling that clung to her day in and day out.

Exactly sixty-two hours and seven minutes after Logan had walked out of her car and into the rain (not that she was counting), Cassie was curled up in a ball in her bed, struggling to deal with an ever-present unsettled feeling, when her phone rang. She moved faster than she thought possible, hoping it might be Logan but knowing there was no way he'd ever talk to her again. She didn't even look at who it was, just swiped the phone open.

"Hello?" she cried, her voice cracking desperately.

"Cassie?" A teary but familiar girl was on the other end of the phone.

Cassie shot up in her bed like she'd been electrocuted.

"Marissa? What's wrong?"

"Can I come over? I really need to talk to you."

All thoughts of Logan were pushed aside in an instinctive reflex of helping her best friend. However, her concern was tainted by lingering annoyance. Seven weeks without a peep and Marissa calls her crying? Cassie wasn't going to make it that easy.

"About what?" she said slowly, sliding off of her bed to start pacing around the room. It was kind of a mess, now that she was the one in charge of cleaning it. Which she most definitely had not been doing over the past few days.

"Sp-Spencer," Marissa sobbed into the phone. She tried to say more, but the words weren't coming out. Cassie held the phone away from her ear for a minute, wondering why Marissa hadn't just sent a text if she was so upset. She'd probably wanted Cassie to hear her crying to make her more sympathetic. With an annoyed huff, Cassie bit back her irritation. Two could play at that game.

Just as she was about to say something dismissive and appropriately rude, she stumbled. Her things were strewn about the room so haphazardly, it could have been anything. But she looked down and it was Logan's green hoodie. The one that he'd let her keep after the Fourth of July. The one he thought she looked really good in. The one she'd been sleeping with in her arms before tossing it aside every morning in a new half-hearted attempt to forget about him.

Tears formed in the corner of her eyes as she scooped it up with one hand and brought it to her nose. It still smelled like him. Everything did, the gingery citrus scent clinging to everything he'd touched, even her sheets. She'd even crawled under her bed to see if the floor smelled like him.

It was definitely getting ridiculous. She needed her best friend. It didn't matter if this was Marissa's big goodbye or some lame attempt to explain herself. Cassie needed to see her. She missed her.

Plus Cassie's house was full of all sorts of tension. Satisfied that Cassie was on their side now, her mom had left the day before, saying there were things to arrange back in Helena before Cassie left for school and in advance of their annual end of summer party. It was only Cassie and her dad again, like it had been in June.

But the mood was completely different. When her dad wasn't off fishing, he was strolling around the house with a satisfied swagger that made Cassie slightly ill to witness. She didn't need Marissa bringing even more drama into her house.

"I'll come to your place," Cassie said. "It's kind of a mess here." It wasn't the best excuse, but Marissa bought it, thanking her before hanging up with another exaggerated sniff.

As Cassie pulled out of her driveway, she worried what she

would say to her former friend once she got to her house. Everything that had happened seemed so far away now. Had it really only been two months since Marissa had driven up to visit with Spencer in the car? It felt like years.

Without Logan taking up nearly every waking second of her day, Cassie realized just how alone she was this summer. Her sister was busy with her internship, and wouldn't be back until late August for the big annual golf tournament in the next town over. Their parents hosted another party, even more important than the Fourth of July, because all the players attended. There'd be other families from Helena, just like there had been in July. But in all the weeks that Cassie had been stuck here at the lake, no one from school had reached out to her. She was totally alone.

Sure she got messages and was tagged online in stuff, but she hadn't seen anyone face to face in what felt like months. Was she so forgettable? Without school or cheerleading or any other reason for people to see her, apparently she wasn't as important as she thought she was. Maybe they'd all seen through the fake facade as well, and now that high school was over, they didn't have to pretend that they actually liked her anymore.

Maybe she needed Marissa back in her life for more than one reason.

"Cassie, I am so sorry!" Marissa fell into Cassie's arms the second she opened the door. While she was happy to hear it, the gasping sobs coming from Marissa seemed a little over the top.

"Hey, it's okay," Cassie said, patting Marissa's back. She'd already decided to accept whatever Marissa presented as an excuse. "I get it. He's hot. I dumped him. He was fair game."

"I got what I deserved. He dumped me!" She dissolved into a slobbering mess right before Cassie's eyes.

Steering Marissa towards her bedroom, Cassie held back the

tiny bit of glee at this unexpected revelation. But she quickly turned her focus to her miserable friend. If this had been any other boy, what would she do?

"Pit stop," Cassie said, and steered her into the kitchen to grab a pint of ice cream from the freezer. She didn't even look to see what it was; all that mattered was it contained the sweet sugary coldness that would soothe the worst kinds of pain.

Curled up on Marissa's bed, Cassie waited patiently for the crying to stop, smoothing back her friend's dark curls from her face. It took another few minutes, but finally the sobs quieted, and she took a few gasping breaths before launching into the story.

"I should have gone with you that night at the restaurant," Marissa started. Despite her resolve to forgive her no matter what, Cassie didn't offer any sign of disagreement at this declaration. "We went out to some house party. It was super boring but I was just so happy to be with him, without you around. What a bitch thing to do."

"Well, it wasn't the nicest thing you've ever done," Cassie acknowledged, trying to keep her tone light but the hurt still shining through.

Marissa looked up at her with red-ringed eyes.

"We made out on a couch, but he was so drunk, it was like kissing a fire hydrant." She gave a shudder. "He fell asleep; he was totally out of it. I had to drive him home in his car and then call my mom to come pick me up. She was super pissed."

"Sounds about right," said Cassie. Though when she'd been in those situations she'd avoided any parental involvement, thanks to Marissa.

"But my mom was kind of happy to hear that it was Spencer." That also sounded familiar. "She didn't really punish me, and when he came over the next day to apologize, my mom let me go out with him that night."

"Spencer, apologize?" That was not something Cassie had ever experienced.

"I know, right? He was being so sweet at first. I thought..." Marissa sat up and started blinking back more tears. She looked down at her hands. "I thought maybe it was because he liked me better than you."

Cassie took a deep shaking breath.

"I wanted him to like you better than me, too," she admitted. "I've been trying to get you together for months."

At this, Marissa stopped crying and looked up, her eyes wide with shock.

"Why?"

Cassie shrugged.

"I knew how much you liked him. I was kind of over being his girlfriend after about two months of it. I thought you would be better together and we could all still hang out."

"You mean you'd really want to hang out after we..."

Cassie gasped.

"You didn't!"

Marissa nodded miserably, hand covering her mouth. Tears started to form again in her eyes.

Well this conversation just got a little awkward.

After hearing Cassie complain for so many months of putting off Spencer's requests for more, she wondered if Marissa had figured that's what would keep him interested. It broke her heart a little to think it was probably true. Marissa did what people expected of her, too.

"I'm not mad!" Cassie said, trying to reassure her. "Really! Just surprised. Was it...everything you wanted it to be?"

Marissa shrugged and wiped her nose with the sleeve of her hoodie. It was stained and the sleeves were baggy, like she'd been wearing the same clothes for days. Cassie looked down at her own messy ensemble of old leggings and a huge Stanford sweatshirt she'd swiped from her sister's closet and started to laugh.

"What's so funny?" Marissa asked with a hopeful smile.

"Look at us! We used to never even let anyone in our bedroom if we weren't fully made up and our clothes perfectly matched!"

Marissa looked down at her baggy sleep shorts and unshaved legs. She let out a giggle.

"Practice for college, I guess?"

Cassie laughed harder.

"The clothes or the breakups?"

"Both?" Marissa sniggered. Cassie hugged her tight.

"See, we don't have to go to the same college to go through this kind of stuff together. I'll still be here for you, even when I'm in New York."

Marissa nodded and returned the hug. Cassie handed her a spoon and the ice cream, now nice and melty after waiting patiently on the side table for them to finish talking.

"Here's to college being different!" cried Marissa, clinking her spoon with Cassie's. "No more setting our alarm at 5 a.m. to look perfect for assholes who don't even care about us!"

"Hear, hear!" said Cassie, as they both dug in.

As the ice cream slowly disappeared, Cassie felt her heart start to mend. It was still broken beyond repair in so many ways, but at least this tiny part of it that belonged to her best friend was on its way to being whole again.

CHAPTER TWENTY-EIGHT

THE BAR WAS slow that night, and Logan hated it. A busy bar kept his mind off of other things. Painful things. Also, a busy bar meant lots of tips. Whenever there was just a few people he always hovered and got a little weird, and no one liked to tip weird bartenders.

Tonight there were even less people than usual; only one silver-haired man sat at the end of the bar, swirling a straw around his empty margarita glass.

Mitch Huntington.

Logan had seen him before, both here at the lake and around Helena. Of course he had no idea who Logan was. He'd never given much thought to Mr. Huntington as anything other than just the dad of another rich kid at his high school. Of course, that was before Cassie had entered his life and turned everything upside down. She never talked about Spencer much when they were together, other than passing references to parties or things they'd done together. Logan had been crazy jealous anytime she mentioned his name, but tried to reassure himself she had picked him, so she obviously didn't care about how popular Spencer was, or how rich.

But she'd never actually picked Logan; she'd been told to hang out with him. By her jerk of a father. For all Logan knew, maybe her dad had even asked her to break up with Spencer as part of some larger drama going on with the Huntingtons. What did Logan know about the complicated lives of the wealthy families in his town?

At least now he knew enough to be glad that he'd escaped. He should be grateful to Cassie for breaking his heart. She'd saved him from a lifetime of always feeling like he wasn't good enough and reminders that he wasn't a part of her world.

Luckily, Logan had enough practice at hiding his emotions to not let on to the thunderstorm raging in his mind and served Mr. Huntington like he would anybody else.

Of course, when Mr. Huntington got a call and put the phone to his ear, Logan decided it might be a good time to clean that side of the bar one more time.

"Jason! How are things going? Did that lawyer ever call you back?"

Logan's heart sped up. Jason Hart?

He told himself didn't care. He shouldn't care. This was between his mom and her former boss, and had nothing to do with Logan.

He stood there, wiping the same glass, with his back to the bar.

"Oh yeah? What did the lawyer say?"

A lengthy pause gave Logan's heartbeat the chance to ratchet up another few miles per hour.

"Great news! I knew they'd find something to work with. She'll never see a penny, will she?"

Logan nearly crushed the glass he was holding; he was gripping it so tightly.

So that was it then. After everything his mom had been through, it would all be for nothing. He didn't care that there wouldn't be extra money for Columbia—he'd never counted on that at all. But it made him red with rage to think that just because she'd stood up to someone richer and better connected than she was, it had been a lost cause from the beginning.

The two men started talking about the upcoming golf tournament in town and Logan breathed slowly through his mouth to quiet his racing heart. When he heard Mr. Huntington hang up the phone, he turned around with a practiced smile.

"Anything else for you, sir?"

Mr. Huntington stood up and shook his head, his eyes not quite focusing as he patted his jacket pockets for his keys. Of course he only left a dollar tip for the three drinks he'd ordered.

Logan hoped the drunk idiot crashed his car.

He shook his head. No, that might hurt someone else. Hot anger flared again as he thought of Cassie's lie.

However, it flared less brightly than it had a week ago. He could be furious at someone like Mr. Huntington for driving drunk and hurting someone. But Cassie had been trying to avoid that. She hadn't even been drinking that night; she'd been the one trying to get her drunk friends home safely. He could just picture what a moron Spencer probably was when he was wasted. He must have grabbed the wheel or something idiotic like that. It probably hadn't even been Cassie's fault she swerved.

But it was her fault that she hadn't told Logan right away.

Hideki kept telling him it wasn't that big of a deal.

"Yes but she lied about it," Logan said for the hundredth time as they pounded away at *Call of Duty* later that night. The bar had been so slow, he'd actually left early and he didn't have any houses to clean the next day. They'd started an epic battle that would probably go all night. One more thing checked off from the BSE list.

"So what? Everyone lies," said Hideki, his eyes glued to the screen as one of his players blew up one of Logan's.

"She almost killed me!"

Logan glanced over to see his cousin roll his eyes.

"Pretty sure she made up for that times, like, a million."

"But she lied about it," Logan repeated, attacking Hideki with a supercharged round. "And she let me think she was this nice, funny, perfect..."

Logan shook his head.

"I should have known better than to trust someone like her."

"Someone like what? With money?"

Logan grimaced. Is that what he'd meant?

"You're such a snob, Logan. Get over yourself." He'd earned another eye roll.

"Easy for you to say! You've never had to see your mom counting pennies to be able to go grocery shopping. You've never been the poor scholarship student at school, the only one to ride a bike wearing thrift store jeans in a school full of beamers and Ralph Lauren polos..."

Hideki held up a hand in defeat, his other hand still tapping away at the controller.

"Hey you know we're always here to help. You just need to ask."

"Well, thanks, but I don't need help anymore. I got into Columbia on my own, I'll make enough this summer, take care of me and my mom... Yes!" He finally found Hideki's hidden soldier and blew him up. He turned triumphantly to his cousin, grinning like crazy.

Hideki just looked at him, eyebrows raised as he threw the game controller on the floor in defeat.

"Logan, seriously? She'll be fine. You know my mom will look out for her. You don't need to worry about her."

Logan frowned. Of course he worried about her. She was his mom.

Hideki sighed.

"Look, you can be mad at Cassie, also known as the hottest girl you will ever make out with in your life," he said. "I get that. Sort of. But don't keep living your life just for your mom. You'll be thousands of miles away. This is your shot."

Logan remembered the last time someone had said that to him. Cassie hadn't wanted him to stay behind because of his mom either. Everyone was pushing him to go, but what if he wanted to stay right where he was?

"Maybe I can defer a year, save a little more, wait until things have settled down."

Hideki's mouth dropped open.

"You did not just say that."

"What? It's my life, I can do what I want with it."

His cousin shook his head.

"That's not how this works. You don't work for years then just throw it away because some girl broke your heart."

"This isn't about Cassie! It's about my mom."

"Yeah, okay." Hideki snorted. "It's a big city, you don't have to see her if you don't want to."

Logan's stomach twisted into a tight knot. It wasn't a big city. It was huge. And he'd be all alone. He knew more about it now, that was true, but he'd still have to navigate everything without anyone else there to guide him. He had been so against her help at first, but when he'd opened himself up to it, he realized how little he actually knew. He had poured over her answers to him about New York, keeping track of every little detail she shared about the city. Then, so stupidly, he'd let himself get excited about the idea of having her there with him by his side.

But now that was gone forever. Could he really do it on his

own? Now that he realized how little he knew about the world outside of Montana, he wasn't sure he wanted to go. This wasn't like jumping off a boulder into the lake. This was his future. And then there was his mom's case—though that was apparently all settled now that he'd overheard Mr. Huntington congratulating Mr. Hart. His mom's case was lost and he didn't want to abandon her right when things were going badly for her.

He wished now he'd talked to Hideki about the lawsuit. He couldn't decide if he should tell his mom what he'd overheard at the bar. Would it change anything? She hadn't given him details about where things were with the case, just vague updates about things "moving along." It was late, and it wouldn't do her any good to hear about it in the middle of the night. He sighed and ran his hands through his hair.

"Hey, you don't need to decide anything tonight," said Hideki, putting a hand on his shoulder. "But don't wait too long. Things could get complicated."

Hideki had no idea how right he was.

"Let's just play," Logan said, and gestured for his cousin to pick up his controller.

Hideki bit his lip and started a new game.

If nothing else, at least they could make progress on the BSE list tonight.

CHAPTER TWENTY-NINE

A WEEK after she'd shared the entire pint of ice cream with Marissa and it was finally starting to feel like the summer Cassie had imagined back in June.

No Spencer, hanging out with Marissa at the lake every day, and meeting up with other friends for shopping and coffee in the afternoon. As a twosome they were much more popular than Cassie on her own. With a pang, she thought of how fun it would have been at Missoula with Marissa. Was it really so bad to want to have her best friend by her side instead of heading to New York on her own?

Really on her own.

But then came a suggestion from her newly reinstated best friend.

"A party?" Cassie wrinkled her nose. Marissa had come over to binge another season of *Real Housewives* that morning. "Really? That's what you want to do tonight?"

Marissa nodded firmly.

"My parents' party is tomorrow. Won't that be enough fun for one week?"

She groaned.

"You know that party is super boring. It's only worthwhile because of all the junior tournament golfers. Well, and Di always sneaks us drinks in the kitchen. Let's do something *fun* tonight." Her eyes grew wide at the word fun.

Cassie sighed. She knew what that look meant.

"What if Spencer is there?"

Marissa sniffed and tossed her curls over her shoulder.

"I hope he is. He can see what an ass he was to both of us, and how much better off we are without him."

"I'm not really feeling up—"

"Come, Cass, please?" Marissa turned her big brown eyes at her, hands laced together under her chin. "It'll be fun. It'll mostly be locals anyway. I doubt Spencer will even bother with it. We only have a few more parties like this together."

They'd already missed so much of the summer together. Cassie didn't want to miss any more. With barely a week left until she had to go home and pack up her life, Marissa was right. This could be their last party together this summer.

"Okay, fine." Cassie sighed. "But I'm not wearing anything too skanky. I don't actually want to hook up with anyone." It had been nine long and painful days since that final kiss from Logan, and when she closed her eyes at night, she could still feel his lips on hers. She wasn't ready for anyone to take that away from her quite yet.

Marissa stuck out her lower lip.

"But it's always so much better when we both look amazing. The guys, like, flock to us like moths to a flame."

Cassie shook her head.

"Not interested."

"Come on, it'll help you get over Spencer to flirt a little!"

Cassie's stomach lurched. She'd let Marissa think she'd eaten half a pint of ice cream because of Spencer, and hadn't even mentioned Logan's name. Marissa had been so honest with her; could she bear to admit everything she had felt for Logan?

Just more proof what they'd had was based on lies and Cassie hadn't deserved whatever brief period of happiness she'd had with him. If she'd really cared about him, wouldn't she have wanted to let her best friend know?

But that would have meant telling Marissa what she'd done. In her car. While she didn't really expect Logan to take her to court for it—though she wouldn't have blamed him if he did—the less people that knew about it, the better.

Cassie must have taken too long to reply for Marissa.

"Seriously, Cass, what's the issue? You seem really bummed out. Is this really still all about Spencer?"

She shook her head. Though she wasn't ready to talk about Logan with anyone, there was one thing she'd found out this week that she could share with her best friend...

"My parents are getting a divorce."

Saying it out loud for the first time was unexpectedly painful, and she felt tears rise to her eyes.

Marissa gasped as her hands flew over her mouth.

"I had no idea! They looked so happy at the Fourth of July party."

Cassie bit her lip. They always looked happy to the outside world. Hell, she looked happy to the outside world, and her hurt cut so deep that she was surprised she wasn't leaving a trail of blood behind her when she walked. But she'd learned from the best how to fake it.

"It's a whole mess. She left right after the party, but apparently they talked about it. Like, nine days ago they said it was fine." She tried not to think about it as 'her last night with Logan' but that's what it would always be to her.

"But it turns out they were still fighting. Then Dad got this lawyer and threatened to not give her a penny if she left before this big real estate deal that's happening next month and I don't know what's happening anymore!"

She put her head in her hands.

"Cass, I'm so sorry!" Marissa folded her up in a hug.

"Their party tomorrow is really important." She remembered the worried voice of her sister when she'd called a few days ago with the news about the current uncertainty of her parents' marriage. Cassie had been upset her dad hadn't told her himself. After all, it was still just the two of them at the lake house.

But was she really that surprised at this point? Her parents were world class experts at hiding things from her.

"We have to be there and we have to look like a family. I really messed up on the Fourth of July when I wasn't there."

"We'll still be there tomorrow! With bells on!" Marissa cried, throwing her hands in the air and waving them around for emphasis. Cassie laughed, distracted momentarily from her pain by her ridiculous best friend. "But that doesn't mean we can't go out tonight. We won't stay that late, I promise."

Cassie raised an eyebrow.

Marissa grinned and held up two fingers.

"I swear! Scout's honor! We've been cooped up all week. Coffee doesn't count as going out. We've done the moping, now let's get out there."

It *would* be nice to do something other than sit around at home or coffee shops, Cassie thought. It might even be fun to dance a little.

"Okay, fine." She sighed, but couldn't help but smile as soon as she saw how happy she'd made Marissa.

Now if only there was a way for Cassie to be that happy and the night would be perfect.

THE AIR OUTSIDE was so cold that going into the house was like walking into a furnace. The room pulsed with music and moving bodies. Cassie felt uneasy at the familiarity of it all. How many nights had started like this? The same droning music, the same boring people, the same watered down drinks. This wasn't what she'd wanted this summer at the lake, yet here she was. A long, tired sigh escaped her lips and floated into the chilly night air. This was what she was supposed to be doing with her life apparently. Nothing had changed.

Then why did she feel like she had lost everything?

The second she walked in, she felt all eyes on her. Had it really been that long since she'd been out? She recognized a good number of the people here, at least their faces. They were mostly locals as Marissa had promised, but there were a fair amount of kids from school there, too. Too many for Cassie to really feel comfortable. News of Spencer's summer had made the rounds on social media and without the hallways of Helena Prep to help spread her own version of events, she'd been cut off from people. They'd filled in the gaps however they'd wanted.

"Whose party is this, anyway?" Cassie asked, looking around at the house. It was more modern than hers. More like Spencer's, or the ones she'd visited with her dad earlier in the summer. All open space and sleek furniture. This much white leather made her anxious, but hey, it wasn't her problem if things got trashed.

Marissa shrugged.

"Brittney something, I think? My dad knows her dad."

Brittney's dad knew everybody, it seemed. She resisted pulling up Instagram to look at the photos that Brittney had posted of Logan she may or may not have saved. Had that really been just two months ago? Cassie had deleted all the others on her phone in a fit of paranoia and depression, worrying that somehow her parents would see them and make more trouble for him.

The Harts had already caused the Hanes enough pain for one summer.

Cassie looked around at the throbbing crowd. It took her about three seconds to locate Spencer, in the immediate vicinity of the keg in the kitchen. Neither Marissa nor she felt the need to have beer, but there were plenty of other things floating around.

She had gone months without getting drunk. She'd promised her parents at the beginning of the summer...

Screw them, she decided. They'd promised to love each other forever, and look how that had turned out. Besides, she'd already tried to change herself into someone better and it hadn't made a difference. What was the point of pretending otherwise?

Three shots later, and she'd started to forget why she hated parties like this. They were kind of fun, once you didn't really know what was going on around you.

She'd managed to lose Marissa at some point, and fell onto a couch, her bare thighs sticking to the leather as her eyes roamed back and forth around the room, trying to find her best friend. But that made her dizzy, so she closed her eyes and leaned her head back.

"You about ready for bed, princess?" Her eyes shot open at the all-too-familiar voice of Spencer next to her. He slid his arm around her shoulder and was smiling at her as if she'd been there at his side all night.

Had she been at his side? She looked around. Wasn't this the same party she'd been to a thousand times?

She shook her head. No, she had come with Marissa, who was heartbroken over the guy currently grinning at her like the cat who'd caught a big juicy mouse by the tail.

"After what you did to Marissa, you really think that'll

work?" She crossed her arms and glared at him. He only smiled wider and handed her the drink in his hand.

"I realized she could never be you." He leaned in close, his breath hot on her neck. Cassie's skin crawled and her stomach lurched. "No one compares to you, Cass. Look around." He gestured to the room. Cassie's eyes darted around and her breath caught in her throat.

Logan was standing in a corner, his arm around Brittney, the ever-so-gracious hostess. Cassie's stomach burned at the thought of this being another Instagram moment for her. *Finally scored a kiss with the cute waiter!* would accompany an adorable selfie of the two of them, announcing to the world what Cassie was witnessing right before her eyes. The shots in her stomach swirled around, ready to make a reappearance.

She turned her attention back to Spencer.

His lips were parted in a lewd smile, his eyes slowly lingering over her low top and short skirt. A year ago, that look would have sent her heart fluttering. But it had been months since it had done anything other than annoy her. Now it just creeped her out and pissed her off.

She smiled up at him, and batted her eyelashes. He leaned in close, as his arm tightened against her shoulders. Just when his lips were inches from hers, she dropped the cup she'd been holding right into his lap.

"Oopsie!" she cried, as he jerked back and cursed. A giant wet spot had appeared on his crotch, staining his jeans dark.

"What the hell, Cassie?" He stood up and glared down at her. She sniggered as she realized what a perfect shot it had been. A few girls standing around them joined in as she laughed, pointing to what was clearly proof Spencer had just peed his pants. Cassie hoped Marissa was somewhere close and able to see it.

His eyes flashed and his hands clenched at his sides. Cassie knew he wouldn't do anything to her, not in front of so many people, but she controlled her laughing anyway. She stared him in the eyes and shrugged.

"Sorry, I guess I'm not what you thought I'd be."

"This is the last time you embarrass me like this, you bitch," he hissed before stalking off out the front door. She knew he always kept clothes in his car so he could change before getting home and avoid smelling too much like smoke and beer, so it wasn't like he'd have to stay like that all night. He was overreacting just a tad, but if he'd been at the party since it had started, he was probably way drunker than she was.

Marissa plopped down next to her.

"That. Was. Amazing," she said in a slightly higher than normal voice. Her eyes shone with heady mixture glee and tequila. "Totally worth coming out, right?"

Cassie nodded, though slightly less enthusiastically than her friend. If things really were over between her parents, her dad would still need Mr. Huntington's help to keep his business running, and pissing off Spencer probably wasn't going to make things easier for him.

"Come on, let's dance." Marissa was pulling her off the couch. "Really show him what he's missing."

As she turned to head out into the yard where the DJ had set up, Cassie stole a glance back at Logan, to see if he'd witnessed Spencer's little tantrum. Her heart sank as she spotted the back of his head, still engrossed in his conversation with Brittney.

He'd never even noticed she was there.

CHAPTER THIRTY

SOME STUPID HOUSE party that Hideki had been invited to was not how Logan wanted to spend his night off. But his cousin had reminded him of their promise at the beginning of the summer.

"BSE! Best summer ever! Say yes to everything."

So far they'd managed to knock off another few things from their list. With only a little over a week to go before he had to head back to Helena, time was running out. Of course, he could always stay longer, and put off school. Hideki hadn't totally convinced him he didn't have to stay. But somehow he had convinced Logan to go out tonight.

At least it would let him see what a 'real party' at Columbia might look like. Hideki had been to tons this summer, and promised they were all the same. Logan still couldn't think of the city without seeing Cassie there next to him, but maybe tonight, surrounded by so many other people, he could finally get his mind off of her. Maybe he could start to see a future in New York on his own.

It had been nine days since his phone had lit up with a message from her but it felt like months. He couldn't bear to delete their conversation, so he would see the counter every day, telling him exactly how long it had been since the last message. 5 days. Then 6. Now almost 2 weeks.

This would end tonight. He was moving on.

The second he walked in to the party, however, he regretted it. This was not the way to forget about Cassie; all he saw were copycats. The same long blond hair, the same expensively frayed cutoffs and designer hoodies worth more than he made in a week. They all looked like her but not one could even hold a candle to her.

The beautiful, lying, rich girl who'd broken his heart.

"Hey guys, glad you could make it." One of the copycats came up to them. Logan thought her name might be Brittney. He remembered singing her happy birthday at the restaurant earlier in the summer.

She started talking to him, and Hideki caught the eye of someone he knew from the boat shop and wandered off. Logan's pulse quickened at the thought of talking alone with Brittney; he had no idea what to say. But she seemed happy to chatter away, her hand lingering on his arm. All he had to do was nod and smile.

At some point Hideki shoved a cup into his hand as he passed by, and Logan didn't even look to see what was in it. He drank it in a few gulps. Brittney laughed and said something about bartenders being the best drinkers. He'd laughed at that too, and she beamed. His heart gave the tiniest flutter. Maybe he just had to give someone else a shot in order to start getting over Cassie. Logan ran a hand down Brittney's arm, just to see what it felt like.

Nothing. Not even the hint of a spark.

Someone walked by with a tray of shots. He took two and downed them both.

"Woah, Logan, slow down!" said Hideki over the music. When had he shown up again?

Logan shook his head with a glance towards Brittney.

"Best summer ever, right?" he yelled back. Brittney flashed him a grin that showed all of her perfect white teeth. Her tank top was so low he could see the top of her bra.

"Yeah, but not if you can't remember it."

Logan didn't want to remember.

Everything he'd been holding in so carefully, so that Hideki and his aunt and uncle wouldn't know the pain he was in, was bursting free tonight. Seeing what life would be like for him, without Cassie at his side, was painful and depressing and no amount of Brittney's bra showing would fix that. But he didn't really have any other options.

He took a third shot for good measure.

It felt good to be numb. He forgot everything. He laughed at Brittney's not very funny jokes, and let her lead him outside, where he danced with her, letting his arms drape over her hips as she shimmied close to him. His stomach did a funny flip at one point. It wasn't a spark, not even close to what holding Cassie in his arms had done to him. But it was something. And maybe it could help drown out everything else he was feeling right now.

And then he saw Spencer.

A rage Logan hadn't felt since the night he'd yelled at Cassie's dad boiled up inside of him. Spencer was standing at the door to the house, a cocky grin on his face, an arm slung over the shoulder of a tiny redhead with a giant chest. The complete opposite of Cassie's tall and lean curves.

No. Logan shook his head. He wasn't thinking about her tonight. He turned his attention back to Brittney gyrating in front of him. But his eyes kept glancing back over her shoulder to Spencer, and Cassie wormed her way to the front of his mind again. How could she not, with her ex standing right there, his smug face just asking to be punched?

Logan leaned into Brittney and told her he needed to find the bathroom. She waved in the direction of the house, spouting off its location but he wasn't paying attention. He kept his eyes trained on Spencer, formulating a rough semblance of a plan as he approached. Hideki appeared at his side with a drink, but backed off when he saw who Logan was staring at.

"Just let me know if you need back up!" he shouted over the music, and shoved a cup into Logan's hand.

He weaved his way closer, slowly, so he didn't spill his drink. His legs felt heavy and the music had gotten louder all of a sudden.

Then Spencer suddenly glared in his direction. Logan's heart started beating faster as he prepared for a confrontation. But as he kept walking, he realized Spencer wasn't looking at him, but through him. He moved to the right a little, and Spencer's gaze didn't shift. Logan looked around, now relatively sure that he wasn't the intended target.

There, behind him. There she was. Cassie.

Logan turned away, his fuzzy mind not even able to process what he was seeing. She looked even better than he remembered. Her silky top hugged every curve and the skirt she had on was the shortest he'd ever seen her in. He remembered that none of it was for him, and he most definitely hated her, but yearning tugged at his bruised heart.

Spencer was still glaring at her, a dark look in his eyes. Logan had to hold back a laugh. What did Spencer have to be pissed about? He had everything he could ever want, while Logan got nothing.

When Spencer made a move in Logan's direction, he shrank back into the crowd. Had he spotted Logan after all? Did he even remember who he was? He probably only registered as 'that waiter who didn't served me alcohol' on Spencer's radar.

Cassie was talking to some guy, a tall beefy looking dude who must have been at least twenty-one. Logan wouldn't have dared to card him if he'd ever been to the bar. But he didn't seem like the type to frequent Chez Pierre. His huge motorcycle boots over ripped jeans and leather jacket looked very out of place in the midst of all the Hollister and American Eagle. Logan had worn his best shirt and still felt like trash, but this guy didn't even seem to notice anyone else, much less care what they thought of him. All his attention was focused on the blonde in front of him. Cassie threw her head back and laughed at whatever he was saying.

So she didn't care about people seeing her out with someone like this guy, but she'd snuck around with Logan. The final knife twisted in his already shredded heart and he turned to go. But a movement from Spencer caught his eye. He was approaching Cassie from behind, a fierce look in his eyes.

Logan shifted on his feet, ready to...to do what exactly? Go save a girl who clearly didn't care about him? Who'd lied to him and had been too embarrassed to be seen in public with him?

Spencer sidled up next to Cassie, his hand poised over her drink. Logan narrowed his eyes as Spencer slipped one hand around her shoulder and the other dropped something into her cup. She turned to look up at him, not even noticing her drink, her eyes flashing anger.

Spencer help up his hands, and Logan could hear his loud defense from where he stood.

"Hey, just trying to be nice. Looked like you were in need of saving."

Logan couldn't hear her response, but she rolled her eyes and turned back to beefy-motorcycle-boots guy. Her cup was still at her side, and Logan held his breath, waiting to see if she'd take a drink.

Should he stop her?

Her laugh ringing across the lawn gave him the answer he needed. She was doing fine on her own. She'd been to parties like this before, and would keep going to them long after she'd forgotten all about him. This was her world, not his.

Let her deal with the consequences herself.

Logan turned on his heels and went to go find Hideki. He was ready to go home.

CHAPTER THIRTY-ONE

"WATCH OUT!" Marissa shrieked and stumbled into Cassie, knocking her drink out of her hand.

As if this night could get any worse. Cassie looked down at her silk top, now totally drenched. The guy she'd been talking to cursed about the two tiny drops that had fallen on his boots, and Cassie rolled her eyes. He hadn't been that interesting anyway, but he'd started talking to her and she couldn't help but be polite as she'd been taught. And he had been kind of funny, but the multiple shots she'd done probably had more to do with that than any innate humor he might have possessed.

As the guy walked away, still cursing, a giggling Marissa clung to her, drunker than Cassie had seen her in ages. But then again, she hadn't seen her at all in weeks, Cassie reminded herself.

She hugged her best friend back, trying to be happy about having at least one thing going right in her life.

So what if she'd caught Logan looking at her with more hatred in his eyes than she'd ever seen on a person? New York was a big city and Columbia was a big school. He clearly realized he had options, thanks to the ever-attentive Brittney, and wasn't wasting any time moving on.

And so what if Spencer was officially the most douchey person on the planet? He couldn't even stand to see her talking to another guy. 'Saving' her is what he'd said. Cassie snorted as she thought about his lame excuse to try yet again to claim what he still saw as his territory. She wished now she'd have thrown her drink on him for the second time that night, and avoided ruining one of her favorite tops.

At least she hadn't slept with him, she reassured herself. Poor Marissa would be dealing with that emotional fallout for a while. For the handful of days they had left together, Cassie was determined to support her best friend in any way she could.

But not if that meant standing around drinking cheap alcohol and talking to random guys.

"Let's go," she said. "I'm totally over this party."

Marissa nodded, her eyes bright.

"Let's get food!" she declared. Cassie sighed, but smiled. She was so happy to have Marissa back in her life she'd gladly take her drunk ass anywhere she wanted.

Except for the tiny fact Cassie was about five drinks too wasted to be able to drive either.

"Who's driving?" she yelled over the music, wondering if Marissa even remembered driving here in her little red VW. There was no way Cassie was driving that thing, not in this state, and not ever again, she'd decided. No need to tempt fate.

Marissa looked at Cassie in confusion. Clearly she didn't realize quite how drunk they both were. Cassie sighed and tried to find someone who looked familiar in the crowd. There were faces she knew from school, from her summers at the lake, but who did she trust? With a pang, she thought of the last time she'd been at a party and wanted to escape and she'd called Logan.

But she wasn't thinking about him. That was over. Brittney could have him.

After another final scan of the room, she realized she'd have to call her sister. It wasn't that late, but she knew she'd get an earful in the morning.

What were sisters for?

"CASSIE THERE'S someone here to see you," Di called at her bedroom door barely 7 hours after Cassie's head had hit the pillow. She groaned and rolled over. She'd been having a very nice dream about an afternoon she'd spent with Logan at the lake. Waking up and realizing it would never happen again was like a cold shower on a winter night.

"Who is it?" It couldn't be Marissa or she would have just come right in herself. Then she remembered Marissa had slept over and was in the guest room. That brought a smile to her face.

"He says his name is Hekiki or something."

"Hideki!" she said, and shot up in bed, her smile vanishing. She shot a glare at her sister. "It's not that hard of a name."

"Whatever." Di rolled her eyes. "He's waiting outside. I thought it best he not come in. Dad might think he's the new landscaper." Cassie glared at her sister as she floated out of her room. Had her family always been this awful? Or was she only just now realizing the extent of their messed up priorities?

Cassie jumped out of bed and ran to the front hall, in her rush not even bothering to put a robe over her thin tank top and sleep shorts. She flung open the door and shivered a little in the cold morning air. She couldn't wait for a proper summer on the east coast with months of heat instead of a few measly weeks.

"Hey, Cassie," he said, wide eyed as he took in her sleep-wear. He cleared his throat. "Sorry-not-sorry to wake you up."

Cassie huffed in frustration and crossed her arms over her chest. She stepped back from the door, and he followed her into the entryway.

"What is it?" She ran through the possibilities of why he might be there. Had she forgotten something at their house he was only returning now? At 8 a.m. the day after a party? That was just rude.

Or maybe Logan had a message for her? Her heart started racing.

"Does Logan..."

Hideki shook his head.

"He's, uh, not doing too great. He doesn't know I'm here, actually. He's in the hospital."

The floor must have dropped out from under her, because Cassie could barely stand.

"What? Why?" She leaned against the wall for support, her legs refusing to support her.

"Spencer beat the crap out of him last night."

"Oh, my gosh!" She took a deep shuddering breath, her stomach threatening to release last night's shots.

That must have been Spencer's big plan for revenge for her. But he didn't know she'd been with Logan. Who could have told him?

"He thought something happened to you, that Spencer did something."

Cassie's heart fluttered. He'd been protecting her? From what? She frowned.

"Why would he think that?"

"It's a little complicated." Hideki flushed. "I'll let Logan explain it though. I can drive you over if you want. I mean, if you want to see him."

"Of course I want to see him! Let me just change."

"Cassie you can't go see him."

She turned and saw her dad standing in the hallway, blocking the route to her room.

"I'll just...wait outside," she heard Hideki say and a minute later there was the sound of the front door slamming. Cassie still hadn't taken her eyes off her father.

"What do you mean I can't go?"

"We have the party today. Your mother will be here in an hour. She'll need your help getting ready."

"Di is here."

"We need the whole family together. It's what people expect."

The twist in her heart was familiar. She always did what they expected. She had to.

From down the hall Marissa appeared, bleary eyed and taking in the scene with a frown. Cassie couldn't leave her friend here while she ran off to see Logan. She'd done that once before and it had just started a chain of events that had ended with a broken heart for Cassie and so much worse for Logan.

She shouldn't get involved again. She had to accept things were over. They all expected her to stay and help them. So that's what she should do.

Right?

CHAPTER THIRTY-TWO

EVERY BREATH WAS PAINFUL, but Logan knew it had been worth it to see Spencer bleed. He just wished he hadn't gone quite so far and ended up in the hospital. This was going to cost a fortune.

He took stock of his body. A cracked rib, a re-dislocated shoulder, bruises all over his face and chest, and they'd even had to reset his jaw. Miraculously no teeth had gotten knocked out. He closed his eyes. Going off to Columbia with a few teeth missing was not how he wanted to start his Ivy League career.

In the end, it hadn't saved Cassie though. He'd been too late. Spencer had already done whatever he'd wanted to with her. Or at least, Logan assumed. He hadn't exactly given Spencer the time to explain himself.

He'd wanted to save her so badly. Wanted to prove that he could help her. Even when she'd betrayed him. Why?

With a painful sigh that made his entire body scream, he turned to one side.

Because despite everything, he loved her. He'd been so close to telling her that night when it all ended. It had been easy enough to tell himself he'd imagined feeling that way, that it hadn't been real.

The agony ripping through his heart right now was proof enough that it had been and still was very real.

He'd never forgive himself for not getting there in time.

The panic he'd felt when he'd run back into the sweaty mess of bodies had been like a shot of adrenaline as he searched desperately for her blond head amongst all the others. Brittney had beamed when she'd seen him, but he'd brushed her away.

How could Cassie be gone already? He'd thought. Had she fallen into the water? He'd made his way through the yard to the lake, scanning the dark waves for a body.

Would he ever see her again?

Lying here miserable in a hospital room was what he deserved. He curled up in a ball on his side, the tears that had been collecting there through the pain finally falling.

He heard the door open and quickly wiped them away. It was probably his mom. He didn't want her to feel worse than she already did.

"Logan?"

He whipped his head around and didn't even regret the pain that shot through his head. Cassie was standing there in front of him, her green eyes filled with worry. She was wearing boots with sleep shorts and a giant hoodie, her hair not even brushed.

She'd never looked more beautiful.

"You're okay!" He sat up, and winced. She ran over to the bed and put a hand on his chest.

"Don't get up! Look at you!" she cried. He looked down at her hand and she withdrew it in a flash. He wished she hadn't. The warmth that had started to spread through him at her touch had been like a balm for his countless wounds.

"I can't believe you're okay." He wanted to take her in his

arms, make sure she was really here. He'd been imagining the worst and to have her looking tired but perfectly fine was like the weight of the world had lifted off his shoulders. His bruises and pain seemed worth it a hundred times now, to know that she was safe.

"Of course I'm okay, why wouldn't I be?" Cassie frowned.

Logan bit his lip. He was not proud of what he'd done. The danger she'd been in—because of him.

"Logan," Cassie had on her most serious of faces. "What happened last night?"

"I saw Spencer put something in your cup when you were with that guy in motorcycle boots." He turned away, his face on fire with shame and guilt.

Cassie gasped. He still didn't look at her.

"I was still so mad, and so drunk, I thought you deserved it." He swallowed hard. "I'm so sorry."

"Why are you sorry? He's the one that did it."

She didn't sound mad, amazingly. He peeked over at her. She didn't look thrilled, mostly curious and concerned.

"I would never want anything to happen to you," he said. The relief of seeing her safe was fading, and the lingering pain of his injuries was making it hard to breathe evenly. "I can't believe I thought for even a second that was something anyone deserved. It took about three seconds after I got in the car that I demanded Hideki take me back to the party to make sure you were okay. But you weren't there."

Cassie shook her head.

"I left almost right after Spencer came up to me."

"With who?" Logan cringed. He sounded jealous and he had no right to be.

"Marissa. She spilled my drink all over me so I wanted to go. We were both already pretty wasted. My sister picked us up."

Logan sat back against the pillow and buried his hands in his face. She hadn't even drunk from her cup.

"I freaked out when I didn't see you there. When I got there, Spencer was laughing his ass off with his friends. I thought they did something to you, that you were passed out somewhere and they'd..."

Logan remembered the hot anger coursing through him, giving him the courage to run up to them, and shove Spencer against the wall. He'd landed a few good punches before Spencer had fallen to the ground. It had felt good, to finally have that kind of power over him, to see Spencer cowering beneath him.

It lasted all of three seconds, however, before the other guys had pulled him off and started wailing on him.

Logan had fought back the best he could. Every ounce of frustration had poured out of him and into his fists. But all the righteous anger in the world was no match for four guys at once.

He didn't actually remember even getting to the hospital, but he assumed his cousin must have gotten him here. He hoped it hadn't been his aunt. She'd already put up with enough of his idiocy for the summer.

"I take it you, ah, confronted Spencer?" Cassie said, biting her lip. She was perched on the edge of her chair, leaning in as much as possible without actually touching him. "And it did not go well?"

Logan shook his head, a grin spreading across his face.

"You could say that..."

His shoulders began to shake with the laughter he was holding in. As much as his face and ribs hurt, it felt good to finally have her near. It felt right.

"This isn't funny! He could have really hurt you! And it would be all my fault. Again." Cassie looked stricken, and

Logan stopped laughing. "He should have hurt me. I deserved it."

Logan sucked in a breath, his ribs groaning in protest.

"If anything had happened to you last night, none of it would have been your fault," Logan said emphatically, staring right into her eyes. "It's not okay for people to treat you like that. I'm so, so sorry I put you in danger like that."

Cassie bit her lip as she took in his words.

"I get that but...I still feel like this is my fault," said Cassie, looking at him with her eyebrows drawn together as he shifted in the bed and winced. "I goaded Spencer all night. He was ready to burst and you were there, all set for a fight." She frowned. "Are you taking the medicine the doctor prescribed? Not trying to play it tough?"

Logan rolled his eyes. Even that tiny movement hurt, but to have bossy Cassie back in his life made everything slightly less agonizing.

Wait, was she back in his life?

"Of course it's not your fault," he said, ignoring the medication question. He slid a hand over hers that rested on the edge of the bed. "Spencer was the asshole. I was an asshole for not saying anything. Worse than an asshole, I mean you could have—"

She held up a hand to his mouth. He closed his eyes at the touch of her skin on his lips and breathed her in. That was also painful, but worth it.

"Logan, I'm not mad," Cassie said, and looked away. She worried her bottom lip with her teeth for a minute then took a deep breath. "You're not perfect. Neither am I. And that's...okay."

He raised an eyebrow. She gave a weak chuckle.

"I know, it's not what you'd expect me to say, right?" She shook her head. "But all that pretending to be perfect was just making things so hard. For my parents, for me. I don't want to be that fake person anymore."

A tear fell from her eye and Logan reached up to brush it away. She leaned into his hand and sighed, her breath hot on his skin.

"I know I hurt you, in all possible ways, and you may never be able to forgive me. And that's okay, too. I just...wanted to be sure you were okay."

She stood up, and his hand fell away.

"You're leaving?" his voice cracked.

She hesitated next to the door.

"Do you want me to stay?"

She was giving him the choice. She'd forgiven him but he still hadn't said out loud if he forgave her.

Had he forgiven her?

"How did you get here?" he asked instead.

She stood at the door and blushed.

"Hideki came to see me this morning."

Logan's eyebrows shot up, by far the least painful movement he'd made that morning.

"Hideki's been here for a while," said Logan, not sure why his cousin hadn't mentioned a pit stop at the Hart's lake house before coming to see him with a large to-go cup of black tea. The nurses had immediately taken it away, grumbling about caffeine addictions. "He just left when you came in, actually. Were you waiting in the hall or something?"

She bit her lip and shook her head.

"My dad didn't want me to leave," she said, her voice shaking. "There's this party this afternoon, really important. He... he said if I left to see you, then I should just forget about Columbia. If they couldn't trust me to do one simple thing, they couldn't trust me to live thousands of miles away on my own."

Logan's heart sank at the pain etched across her face. How could someone be so horrible to their own kid?

Logan almost laughed at himself. His dad hadn't been any better.

Cassie walked back into the room and sat down again, this time in a chair further away from the bed. Should he ask her to sit closer? He decided he needed to hear what she had to say first.

"That makes him sound really bad," she admitted, looking down at her hands. "But my parents are under a lot of stress. You heard my mom wanted to leave my dad, but Di just told me he got a lawyer to cut her off completely if she doesn't stay and play the part awhile longer."

A flash of Mitch Huntington sitting at the bar on the phone came to Logan and a pinprick of hope flickered in his heart. His mom hadn't talked about her lawsuit at all lately, and he assumed that meant the worst. But maybe he'd gotten it all wrong...

He brought his focus back to Cassie, staring miserably at her clasped hands.

"That doesn't make him sound much better," Logan said with a frown.

Cassie shrugged.

"Whatever is happening with my parents is their business. But we stick together in our family. It's not unreasonable for them to ask certain things of me in exchange for living the kind of life we do."

Logan raised an eyebrow again. This didn't sound like her. Not the Cassie he knew, at least.

"But you're here? You picked me over your family?"

Luckily he wasn't hooked up to a heart monitor, or she'd have been able to hear his pulse racing as he waited for her reply.

"No," she said, still looking down. His heart deflated in an instant like a burst balloon. "I picked me."

She looked up and her eyes were two fierce green flames.

"I didn't know if you'd be able to forgive me. I spent over an hour crying in my room with Marissa, trying to figure out what to do. She told me to come, but of course she wants me at Missoula with her." Cassie gave a rueful smile. "But what if I came and you didn't want me here? I'd have given up so much for someone who didn't even want me."

But Logan did want her. He cursed his stupid broken ribs for not letting him jump out of bed to show her just how much he wanted her. Instead, he held his breath, waiting for more.

"And then I realized I'm still basing all my decisions on someone else. So what do I want? Do I want to go to the party? Not if it means smiling and pretending everything with my parents is fine, when it's a total drama-fest. Do I want to go to New York? Not alone.

"But...I do want to see you. One last time. Even if you don't—"

"I want you here!" Logan couldn't stand it anymore. He threw off the blankets and swung his legs off the bed, trying to get as close as possible as quickly as possible. "I don't care that you lied. I mean I do but... but it doesn't matter and—ah!"

Logan tried to push off from the bed and a stabbing pain had shot through his abdomen. Cassie rushed over and pushed him back down, choking back something between a laugh and a sob.

"I'm so sorry I lied," she said, tears starting to fall. Her hands were still on his chest, and he put his hands up to brush away tears for the second time that day. "But I'm not sorry I met you."

"I'm not sorry you met me, either," he said with a smile that made his black eye twinge. "I did everything for myself for so long, I didn't think I needed anyone's help. Least of all from someone like you."

"You mean from a rich jerk?" She gave a lingering half-smile that set his heart racing beneath her palms.

"I mean someone so perfect," he said, blinking back tears. She really was perfect, too. "How could you know anything about pain and disappointment and life being hard?"

Her smile fell and she started to pull her hands away.

"But you're so much more than perfect," he said, rushing to explain. "You came to check on me before your dad asked you to. I was the one that pushed you away, and you were just trying to help. All you've ever done is help me. I don't want to push you away anymore."

He leaned up as much as he could, taking her face in his hands.

"I love you," he whispered, as he let his lips gently brush against hers. He heard her soft intake of breath, and held his own as he waited to see what she'd do.

"I love you, too," came her soft reply. She ran her hands up his chest and into his hair, pulling him closer. His ribs groaned in protest, and his shoulder screamed in agony as their lips crashed together again and again.

Totally worth the pain.

CHAPTER THIRTY-THREE

CASSIE WALKED INTO THE BACKYARD, her head held high. She'd spent way too long at the hospital, curled up against Logan in the narrow bed before the nurses had finally come to shoo her away. She made it back home to find the party in full swing and ran up to her room to get ready.

Marissa had been waiting for her with a very helpful pep talk, but Cassie's hands were still shaking as she looked around the backyard. The dress she'd picked out last week for the party now seemed too tight; she could barely breathe. Her heart was pounding, but she told herself even if this was it for her family, she'd still have Logan on her side. She found her parents standing by the French doors leading into the house, greeting people as they milled about.

Her dad's eyes flashed as Cassie stood in front of them.

"I need to talk to you." She spoke softly, but her tone was firm. "Both of you. And Di."

Cassie glanced around and spotted her sister talking to one of the young golfers, but she rushed over when she saw the look Cassie shot her.

As they all followed her into the kitchen, she could feel the annoyance radiating off of them.

"This really isn't appropriate to leave our guests so early in the evening," her mom started, as she turned to face Cassie. With a wave of her hand, the servers and other staff left the kitchen. It was just the Harts now, Cassie facing her sister and parents, her heart beating a thousand miles an hour.

Could she really say this?

She thought of Logan, and the beating he'd taken when he thought he hadn't been able to keep her safe. This couldn't possibly be worse than that, could it?

"I'm sorry I wasn't here earlier," she said, shifting her weight from one foot to the other. "But I had something to take care of."

"You mean that Hanes scum?" her dad spat. "I thought I made it clear that you weren't to see him again."

Cassie took a deep breath. She could do this.

"I'm still a part of this family," she said, looking them all in the eye. "I may not always agree with you, or do things the way you want me to but I still want to make you proud, in my own way."

Her dad scoffed and her stomach lurched. She took another breath and kept going.

"But I can't play these games anymore. I can't keep lying, to myself, to others. I want to go to Columbia. I want to be with Logan. I'm sorry if you're not happy about that. I still love you all. I...I hope you can still love me."

She waited one more breath, then, seeing their angry faces, looked down, her eyes filling with tears.

"Of course we love you," said her mom, and Cassie looked up, her heart soaring. Her mom's eyes were soft for the first time Cassie could ever remember. The facade had slipped a little, and Cassie thought she looked even more beautiful than normal. "I think your father may have been a little hasty this morning in his ultimatum. Things have been tense for everyone lately."

That was probably as close to the truth as she'd ever get, but it was enough to reassure Cassie that her future might be one she could actually look forward to.

"It's just..." Cassie's mom glanced at her dad, whose lips were pursed in furious disappointment. "Things between your father and I aren't quite sorted out. And the lawsuit he's dealing with isn't going the way we'd hoped. So there might not be quite as much for you at Columbia as we'd hoped."

Diana was scowling. That meant less for law school and her California lifestyle as well.

Cassie's face, however, lit up in a wide grin.

"You mean I might have to get a job?" Her mind raced with the possibilities. Maybe she could find a job with Logan! And even if she didn't, she knew he'd be there to help her figure it out. He'd be thrilled to finally be able to share his knowledge of something with her.

"We'll figure out all the details later," said her mom, as the facade slipped back into place once again. "Let's not ruin the party with all this talk of our troubles, okay?"

Cassie followed them out back into the yard, her stomach filled with excited butterflies. She wouldn't have to pretend to be happy—she was positively brimming with joy.

She was still going to New York. Logan would be there with her. And they'd help each other figure things out as they went.

Marissa caught up with her and linked her arm through Cassie's.

"I take it everything went okay?"

All she could do was nod, not able to put it all into words quite yet.

"Great!" Marissa squeezed her hand as they made their way down to the beach. "Hey, I meant to ask you before, who was that guy this morning?" Cassie shot her best friend a questioning look. Marissa's eyes were sparkling. "The one who came to tell you about Logan?"

"Hideki?" Cassie grinned. "Logan's cousin? I think I heard he's going to Missoula this year..."

THE COMMUTER RAIL CHUGGED ALONG, the fake leather seats peeling and smelling faintly of smoke. Cassie had spread out her jacket across the seat before sitting down, and now her legs were crossed tight as a corkscrew. She looked around through narrowed eyes, careful to keep her hands firmly on her legs.

Logan couldn't help teasing her just a little.

"I don't think the smell is contagious if you touch something." He raised an eyebrow and smirked.

She rolled her eyes but kept her body as far away from the seats as possible.

"We could have rented a car," she said for the tenth time that morning.

"But it's my first time on a train! Isn't that the surprise?" He grinned. She'd been building up to this surprise for weeks, giving him hints. Six months in New York and this was the first time they'd been to New Jersey. "Or are we going to the Jersey Shore?"

His heart leapt. She'd taken him out to Coney Island one of

their first weekends at school, so he'd already seen the ocean. But he couldn't get enough of it.

Cassie giggled.

"You're adorable when you're excited." She leaned over to give him a quick kiss. He grabbed the back of her head and held her to him, deepening the kiss. He still couldn't get used to being able to do that in public.

"And you're adorable when you're attempting to be thrifty," he said when he finally pulled away.

She flushed.

It turned out the conversation Logan had overheard in the bar that summer hadn't been about his mom's lawsuit, but about Cassie's parents' divorce. It was going to be long and messy, no matter what they'd told her right before she had left for school.

Then, the day after school had started, Logan's mom had called with the news. Hart & Preston had paid out an undisclosed amount to five different women who used to work for them, Logan's mother included. He told Cassie the money had all gone to paying for school, but he hadn't been able to resist getting her a few things for her. It was a nice change to be able to afford more than the basics, but he knew how fast it could all go away. Columbia would last four long years; he wanted to be sure they could enjoy all of them.

Now Cassie found herself on the other side, trying to pay attention to what she spent. No matter what happened with her parents, her trust fund was intact, but she wouldn't have full access until she turned 25. Columbia was turning out a lot differently than she'd pictured. Finding a job had been hard, despite Logan's help, and she always seemed to be short a few dollars at the end of the month.

It had taken her weeks to be able to save enough to get tickets for his surprise.

As they pulled into the station, Logan stood and reached out a hand to help her from her seat. Sneaking in a final kiss, they got off the train and made their way through the crowds and out into the chilly February air.

"This is nothing compared to winter in Montana," he boasted, but he wrapped an arm around her anyway to keep her warm.

"I'm sorry it's not Costa Rica," she said, as she steered them down the street. Her hand found the tickets in her pocket. She shivered a little in the wind.

His brow furrowed.

"Why would I want to be there, when what I love is right here?" He kissed the top of her head as they waited for a crosswalk sign to change.

"I'm not the only thing you love that's here."

She held out the tickets, her hand shaking from a heady mix of cold and excitement.

"The Camden Aquarium, home to the only great hammerhead shark in the US."

His face lit up in a gigantic smile, dimple on full display, making her knees go weak. Thank goodness his arm was already around her.

"I know it's not the same as seeing them in the wild and—"

"Thank you," he said, cutting her off with a soft kiss on her shivering lips. "One day I'll take you to Costa Rica to see them for real."

And she knew he would.

Everything with Logan was for real.

ACKNOWLEDGEMENTS

When I started this writing journey almost two years ago, I thought it would look one way. Through connecting with other authors, it's become so much more than I ever imagined. In writing, I've found support, love, and friendship. Thank you to everyone who reads my books, whatever stage they're at. Every year I say it'll be my best ever, but as long as I have friends and fans asking for more, every year IS the best ever.

ABOUT DAPHNE JAMES HUFF

Daphne James Huff was the least cool kid in her high school wind ensemble, but now gets to hang out with (fictional) cheerleaders all she wants, so things worked out okay for her in the end.

Daphne works in the non-profit sector during the day talking to anyone who will listen, and spends her nights talking to no one while she writes, reads, and does yoga. Sometimes she comes out of her quiet cave to tell stories to her husband, son, and cat.

The cat is the only one who actually listens.

Get your free copies of her short stories at
www.daphnejameshuff.com

Daphne is the co-founder of a podcast and online community
for indie author moms: www.writermomlife.com

The Princes of Prynesse:

A Royal Distraction

A Royal Decision

A Royal Departure

Dreamers Series:

I Dream of Fire: Parts 1 & 2

The Magician's Test

The Devil's Trial

The Nurse's Secret

Sweet Young Adult:

Leah's Song

Home for Christmas

This Summer at the Lake

www.ingramcontent.com/pod-product-compliance
Lightning Source LLC
Chambersburg PA
CBHW021149110726
47900CB00002B/496